Joe's New World

A Me and Mister P. Adventure

Joe's
New World
A Me and Mister P.
Adventure

Maria Farrer

**Illustrated by
Daniel Rieley**

Sky Pony Press
New York

Library of Congress Cataloging-in-Publication Data is available on file.

Cover provided by Oxford University Press
Cover illustrations by Daniel Rieley

Print ISBN: 978-1-5107-3911-6
eBook ISBN: 978-1-5107-3913-0

Printed in the United States of America

To Nick, with thanks.
And to "Team Unlimited Awesomeness"
who taught me what snow is really about!—MF

For Rebecca and Rachel—DR

CHAPTER 1
SURVIVAL AND ARRIVAL

Joe stared out of the window of the plane. Raindrops raced across the glass as the aircraft taxied along the runway, engines roaring, accelerating faster and faster until it lifted into the air and all the noise was replaced by a gentle hum. Joe watched the ground disappear from view. Goodbye to home, goodbye to friends, goodbye to family—except for Mom and Dad; they were with him, of course.

At first the idea of **the big move** to another country had been really exciting and all Joe's friends had treated him like a bit of a superstar. Everyone wanted to talk to him about it and everyone told him how lucky he was. But now, as everything he knew disappeared beneath a layer of cloud, Joe really wished he could swap his life for someone else's, someone whose dad hadn't been given a five-year engineering contract on the other side of the world, someone whose parents had actually asked their one and only son whether or not he minded about leaving home, school, and friends before going ahead and planning the whole move, basically someone who had said no thank you very much but he would rather stay where he was. Instead, Joe was stuck on this plane with parents who seemed to think this whole move was some big adventure. Joe liked adventure, but he wasn't sure he liked this kind of adventure.

Joe took a photo album out of his cabin bag—it was his leaving present from his class at school. On the front the title was written in big capital letters,

"GOODBYE JOE"

and underneath there was a photo with him in the middle and all his friends around him. Inside, each and every page was covered with photos and messages from all his classmates. Tucked into the back was another picture that Joe hadn't seen before. A lump rose in his throat. It was a recent photo of Roly, Joe's little Jack Russell terrier, who was now living with Joe's granny. Someone had drawn a paw print on the back of it and a sad face. The lump in Joe's throat got bigger and made it hard for him to breathe. He looked out of the window and pretended to be interested in the clouds while he wiped away his tears. He needed to cheer himself up so he searched in his bag until he found a sheet of paper. "Joe's ten worst jokes ever," it said. Lame jokes were Joe's speciality. In times of crisis, everyone relied on him to come up with a terrible joke.

He read through them but, although there were some of his favourite ever jokes on the list, right now they didn't make him laugh at all. In fact they made him feel even worse.

"It's exciting, isn't it?" said Dad, giving him a nudge and leaning forward to see out of the window.

Joe wasn't sure how looking out of a window and seeing nothing but thick cloud counted as exciting. And he didn't even want to look at his dad. The plane bumped its way up through the clouds and Joe closed the album, put it back in his bag, and grabbed the screen control. This was going to be a long flight. There'd better be some good films and games. Anything to take his mind off The Big Move and all that went with it.

* * *

Joe and his family were last off the plane and *the lines for passport control were long.*

When they were called forward, Joe watched as the immigration official flicked through the pages in their passports and looked each of them up and down in a most unfriendly way. Bang went the official's stamp onto the passport.

BANG   BANG   BANG

And that was it. They were now officially residents of a new country. By the time they got to the baggage hall to pick up their luggage, the suitcases had already started arriving. Joe watched as bag after bag appeared through a large, rectangular opening high up in the wall. They bumped down a long slide and onto the carousel to join the other cases going round and round. Passengers jostled to grab their bags, heaving them off the conveyor belt and loading them high on trolleys. Mom's blue suitcase was first to appear, then Dad's. Then there was a bit of a gap when nothing appeared at all. It would be just his luck if they'd lost *his* bag, Joe thought.

There was a jolt and suddenly the conveyor belt creaked and sputtered and slowed almost to a stop. A battered brown suitcase clattered its way down the luggage slide and right behind it something huge and white appeared. It teetered at the top of the slide for a few seconds and then tumbled down in a mass of fur and legs, landing in a heap on the carousel.

"Good grief," said Dad. "That's some bag!"

Passengers pushed forward and stared with their mouths open as the humongous ball of white fur began its circular journey around the carousel with the rest of the baggage. It was still to begin with, then it gave a shake and pushed itself into a sitting position, resting one hairy paw on the battered suitcase.

"It's alive!" said Mom, as the animal turned its head this way and that. Passengers gasped and seemed to forget, for a moment, about searching for their luggage.

Joe raced to the far end of the carousel to get a better look. Now that he could see the creature clearly, he knew, without doubt, that it was a polar bear—not an oversized cuddly toy polar bear, but a real, live bear like he'd seen on the TV. It had a big label around its neck saying Mister P. and there appeared to be a matching label on the suitcase. As the polar bear travelled past, it lifted one paw, almost as

if it were waving at Joe. Joe laughed and waved back. Each time the bear completed another circuit, it waved as it got to Joe. Joe noticed that the bear didn't seem to be communicating with anyone else and it made him feel a little self-conscious. People started to look over and raise their eyebrows as if they expected him to *do* something with this unexpected arrival, but as the initial excitement died down, passengers went back to grabbing their luggage until, finally, the crowds melted away and there was nothing left on the carousel apart from the bear and the battered brown suitcase. Joe and his family stood and waited.

"Still no sign of your bag," said Dad, nodding his head up and down as he counted the suitcases. "It seems strange that it's the only one not to turn up."

"It's not strange, it's just *typical*," said Joe. "Why couldn't it be your bag or Mom's bag? Why does it have to be mine?"

"Calm down," said Dad. "It'll arrive any moment, I expect."

But no more luggage appeared. Just a bear and a suitcase … a bear and a suitcase … a bear and a suitcase.

"Let's ask that man over there," said Mom. "He looks like he works here."

A man in a white shirt with a smart badge had approached the bear and was inspecting a large label hanging from the battered brown suitcase.

"Mister P.," he shouted. "Is there a Mister P. here?"

The polar bear looked down its nose at the man and grinned, displaying two smart rows of rather sharp teeth.

The man yanked the luggage label off the suitcase and stepped away. Joe watched as the luggage handler turned the label over and scratched his head. "Are any of you Joe Beechcroft by any chance?" he asked, looking towards Mom, Dad, and Joe.

"Ah, well, um, yes," Dad mumbled as if he wasn't sure if it was a good thing or not to admit that one of them was, indeed, Joe Beechcroft.

"Joe Beechcroft of 44 Pinewood Avenue?" the man continued.

"Yes," said Dad again, sounding even more doubtful. Joe looked at Dad and back at the man.

"I'm Joe," said Joe. "And my suitcase hasn't arrived. Do you know where it is?"

The luggage handler shook his head. "This is all that's left," he said. "One bear and one brown suitcase—and both of them appear to have your name attached to them."

"*My* name?" said Joe, surprised. "Are you sure?"

The luggage handler walked over and held the label out for them all to see.

"I'm afraid the bear is nothing to do with us," said Dad. "There must be some mistake."

"And that definitely isn't my suitcase," said Joe. "Perhaps there's been a mix-up with the labels."

Dad turned to Joe. "This isn't some kind of joke is it? Something your friends from home have cooked up? I mean, why would there be a polar bear with your name on it?"

"Don't ask me," cried Joe. "You were there when we checked in the luggage and I think I might just remember checking in a polar bear."

BER - DUNK

The carousel came to a stop and the polar bear stood up and jumped off, landing on the ground with a hefty thud. It picked up the battered brown suitcase in its teeth and carried it over to Dad's luggage trolley, plonking it on top of the other bags.

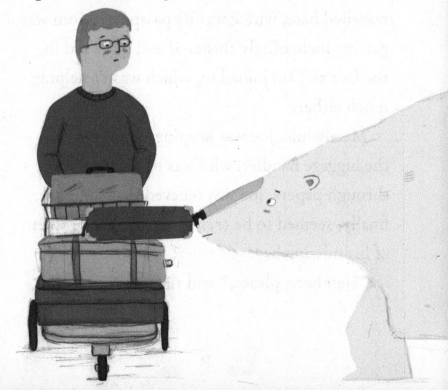

"Hang on a minute!" said Dad. "What are you doing?"

The bear sat down next to the trolley and gave Mom a lick on the cheek with its long black tongue.

"Aaahhhhh!" screamed Mom, and two security guards quickly appeared to assess the situation. Joe assumed that they would arrest the bear and take it away, but they seemed more intent on asking Mom questions about the animal—where did it come from, how had it travelled here, where was its passport? Mom was getting increasingly flustered and quite red in the face so Dad joined in, which wasn't helping much either.

Meanwhile, Joe was keeping an eye on the luggage handler, who was busy checking through papers. Joe was relieved that someone, finally, seemed to be trying to solve the problem of his missing bag.

"Sign here, please," said the luggage handler,

waving a pen and sheet of paper covered in tiny black writing.

As Mom and Dad were still occupied with the security guards, Joe took the form, signed it on the dotted line at the bottom, and handed it back. He was way too tired to read all the small print.

SIGNED FOR BY ....Joe Beechcroft..........

"Very good," said the luggage handler. "He's all yours." The man waved the papers towards the bear.

Joe's eyes widened. "What do you mean, *he's* all mine? *Who* is all mine?"

"The bear, of course. The one you just signed for. And I suggest you get him home as soon as possible. Animals can get a little stressed after a long flight and we don't want any trouble."

Everyone fell silent. Joe looked first at the luggage handler, then at his parents, and then at the bear. The bear didn't look even the tiniest bit stressed. Mom looked stressed, Dad looked stressed, even the luggage handler looked stressed. But Mister P. sat calmly and serenely, resting his chin on top of the pile of suitcases, spreading his lips in what looked like a large grin.

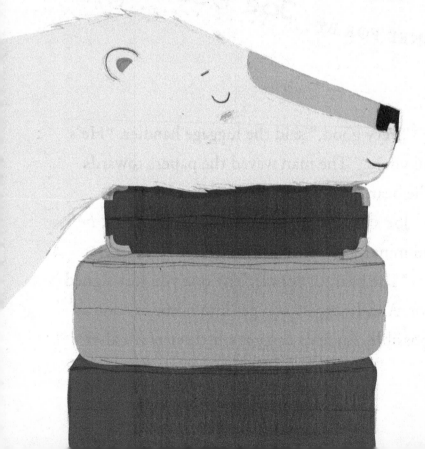

"But what are we supposed to do with him?" said Joe.

The luggage handler held up his hand. "Please keep your voice down. We don't want to cause another security alert."

Dad covered his face with his hands and took a deep breath. "This is all I need," he muttered. "We'll sort the bear out later. Let's just get out of here."

"What about my bag?" said Joe.

"Yes, what about Joe's bag?" repeated Mom. "It's got everything in it. I mean, he hasn't even got a change of clothes."

"You'll need to go and report it missing over there." The man pointed to a desk.

Dad huffed and puffed as he filled in the "lost luggage" paperwork. Joe kept watch over the bear. A smiling lady said she was sure Joe's bags would soon be located and they would be delivered to their house free of charge.

"I should think so, too," said Dad grumpily.

Dad pushed the trolley of luggage towards the exit and the others followed. The strange little group walked quietly through Customs and out into Arrivals: Mom, Dad, Joe, and an extremely large polar bear.

CHAPTER 2
OUT AND ABOUT

A man was waiting, holding a sign high in the air.

BEECHCROFT
FAMILY

it said in large black writing.

"Phew," said Dad, raising his hand and giving the man a small wave. "At least one thing has gone right. The company said they'd send a driver to pick us up and take us to our new home."

Joe quite liked the idea of having a driver, but the word *home* sounded all wrong. How could

Dad refer to this new place as home? Home was where Joe had lived since he was born. Home was where his friends were, where Gran was, where Roly had arrived as a puppy. Joe had seen pictures of the new house and it looked nothing like their old one. It looked strange and new and not like home at all.

"Mr. Beechcroft?" said the man, and Dad nodded. "Welcome! I hope you've had a good flight."

"The *flight* was okay," said Dad. "But we've had a few problems since arriving." Dad glanced in the direction of the polar bear. Mister P. pushed his nose towards the driver and the driver's eyes opened wide and he puffed out his cheeks.

"That's some family pet," he said. "No one mentioned you'd be bringing a bear."

"That's probably because we *didn't* bring him and he's *not* our pet," said Dad, firmly. "There's been some kind of a mix-up, but I thought it would be simpler to sort it all out once we get to the house. He's obviously been sent to the wrong address, so I'm sure someone will be in touch soon enough."

"Well, there's a thing," said the driver and Joe saw him roll his eyes like he thought they were all completely mad. He took the cart from Dad and started pushing it towards the exit doors.

"What I don't get," said Joe, wheeling along beside the driver, "is that I wanted to bring my pet—my actual pet dog—but I wasn't allowed to." He turned to give Mom and Dad his best drop-dead look. "So how come THIS has arrived?" Joe stuck his thumb towards Mister P.

"Search me," said the driver.

"We're going to buy you a new dog, just as soon as we've settled in," said Mom, sounding rather desperate. "That's what we promised, remember? It'll be fun having a puppy again."

"I'd rather have Roly," said Joe, sulkily. "A new puppy will just pee everywhere."

"It's been a long flight," said Dad, sighing. "You'll feel different about things after a good night's sleep."

Dad seemed to think a good night's sleep was the answer to everything. Mom, on the other hand, believed in fresh air and exercise. Joe never slept very well and he wasn't that interested in fresh air and exercise.

They approached the rotating doors to the exit. Mom, Dad, and the driver went first with the cart. Then Joe and Mister P. Joe waited as the door circled and delivered him to the outside. Out in the open, for the first time in hours, Joe flung his arms wide.

"Hello, new world, here I am," he shouted

and got a few funny looks from passersby. The strangeness of it suddenly swamped him and his arms dropped to his sides. The sounds were different, the smells were different, even the air felt different. He closed his eyes and opened them again in case it was just a strange dream.

"I'll go and get the car and meet you here," said the driver. "Luckily I've got the luggage trailer so we should be able to fit the bear in without too much of a problem."

Joe frowned. Where was the bear? He looked back over his shoulder and spotted Mister P. still traveling round and round in the rotating door, blocking anyone else from getting in. Joe tried not to laugh and beckoned for Mister P. to come out. But Mister P. seemed to be enjoying himself. The line of people waiting to use the door got longer and longer and grumpier and grumpier. Round and round and round went the bear.

"If you want a lift, you need to come NOW,"

shouted Joe, as the car pulled up. Mister P. went round one more time then staggered out, looking rather dizzy, and made his way to the back of the trailer.

"Does your bear travel a lot?" asked the driver. "He seems very sure of himself."

Mom, Dad, and Joe looked at each other and shrugged. How were they supposed to know?

Dad helped Joe transfer into the car and loaded up his chair. The driver made sure Mister P. was safe in the trailer before settling himself behind the steering wheel. He turned on the ignition, checked in his side mirror, and pulled out.

Gradually city buildings gave way to more open spaces. The trees were clinging on to their last few fiery leaves of autumn, but the sun was still surprisingly warm.

"I thought you said the weather was going to be freezing," said Joe, pulling off his hoodie.

"Oh, it'll get cold soon enough," said the

driver. "Don't you worry about that. We can go from lovely sunshine straight to snow and ice in a matter of hours. You never know what to expect, so when you live round here it's best to be prepared for the worst."

"Worst like what?" said Joe.

"Blizzards, temperatures way below freezing, ice, wind, power cuts . . ."

"Okay, okay," mumbled Dad. "I think we get the picture."

Mom twisted a tissue in her fingers.

"Sounds cool," said Joe, with just a hint of sarcasm. "If you'll excuse the pun." He turned to look at the bear once again. He wondered if this place may be more suited to polar bears than human beings.

The bear certainly looked quite at home. In fact, he looked as if he was having a great time. His nose was raised to the breeze and his fur streamed out behind him. Joe shook his head. He couldn't quite believe that he was driving along a road in a new country with a polar bear in tow.

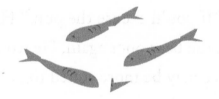

CHAPTER 3
HERE AND THERE

Pinewood Avenue was shaped like a giant lollipop. A long, straight road led all the way to the top where there was a large circular turning area with an island in the middle. All the houses were brand new and almost identical. Joe thought they looked more like log cabins than houses. Each one had a basement level and the ground floor was slightly raised with steps and a ramp leading up to it. Dotted around were tall pine trees with silvery green needles and Joe supposed that's where the name "Pinewood Avenue" came from. Not very imaginative, he

decided as the car came to a stop outside what must be their house.

"Oh isn't it lovely?" said Mom, just a bit too enthusiastically, as she pressed her forehead against the car window. "Just like the photos. I've never lived in a brand new house before."

Dad smiled and took her hand.

"I prefer old houses," said Joe.

"Now, now," said Dad. "Don't be so negative. You haven't even seen inside yet. I've got a feeling you'll be *very* happy when you do."

Joe rolled his eyes. He'd made a decision that no way would he be happy until they did a big move back home. Dad helped Joe out of the car and they watched as the driver opened the back of the trailer and Mister P. backed slowly down.

"I expect he'll disappear off into the woods now," said the driver. "Animals are good at adapting—much better than humans. There's plenty of bears for him to make friends with out there and there's a big lake out the back so he can pick up some fish on the way."

"As long as I don't have to eat fish from the lake," said Joe, making a face. "I hate fish."

"That's a pity," said the driver. "There's a lot of fishing round these parts. Do a bit myself, actually."

Joe smiled. He'd just thought of a good fishing joke. "Do you know why it's so easy to weigh a fish?" he asked.

The driver shrugged.

"Because it has its own scales," laughed Joe.

The driver knitted his eyebrows together in confusion. "You know, like scales," Joe tried again, but the driver shrugged again and seemed to lose interest. Joe shook his head. He wasn't used to people not getting his jokes.

He made his way slowly up the ramp to the front door and waited at the top. Dad took the key out of his pocket, fiddled with the lock, then flung the door open with a big flourish.

"In you go," he said. "It's all yours."

Joe peered around as he went slowly through the door. The smell of wood was overpowering and the building felt like a sweater that didn't fit properly. He turned to see Dad pick up Mom and carry her through the door.

"Welcome to your new home, Mrs. Beechcroft."

Mom giggled and Dad kissed her on the lips.

"Yuck," said Joe as Dad put Mom down.

THUMP   THUMP   THUMP

The house vibrated and all three of them turned to look over their shoulders as Mister P. appeared at the top of the ramp and put his enormous head through the door, dropping his suitcase on the hallway floor.

"Watch out, Mister P.!" said Joe. "Dad might try to kiss you too."

"I don't think so," said Dad, shooing Mister P. out of the door and back down the ramp. "This house is not for bears."

Joe frowned. "What if he's got nowhere else to go?" He leant over and turned the label on the suitcase so Dad could read it. "After all, this *is* the address on his label. The least we can do is let him come in."

Joe Beechcroft
44 Pinewood
Avenue

"Stop worrying about Mister P. and go and explore," said Dad, sounding a little exasperated. "Honestly, he's a bear, he'll be fine. I'm sure he can stand on his own four feet."

It seemed wrong, to Joe, to stop worrying about the bear. Mister P. was now sitting at the bottom of the ramp, his head cocked on one side, looking very dejected. It was bad enough arriving in a new place, but at least Joe and his family had a home to go to. What had Mister P. got? Nothing! Except for an old suitcase— which, come to think of it, was more than Joe had got. Nevertheless, it hardly seemed very fair to shoo the bear away.

Joe sighed and set off to explore the house room by room. Mom and Dad followed him, their eyes on him all the time, watching him expectantly, waiting for some kind of sign that he loved his new home. And the house *was* nice. He couldn't deny it. But he didn't love it.

"Do you want to see your bedroom?" said Mom.

Joe shrugged. He did want to see his room, but he didn't want Mom or Dad to have the satisfaction of thinking he was even the tiniest bit excited. He was determined to let them know just how miserable he was feeling. If he stayed miserable for long enough perhaps they'd change their minds and move back home. Mom and Dad usually did their best to keep him happy.

Mom pointed to a door at the end. "That's yours."

"Wow!" he exclaimed as he went in. He couldn't help himself. This was about twice the size of his room at home. There was a huge window that looked out over the backyard and on to the lake and mountains beyond. There was a TV, a games console, and some speakers. There was an electric guitar on a stand, just like the one he had at home. Someone had done everything they could to make this perfect for him.

"What d'you think?" said Dad as he walked around opening and closing closets and drawers.

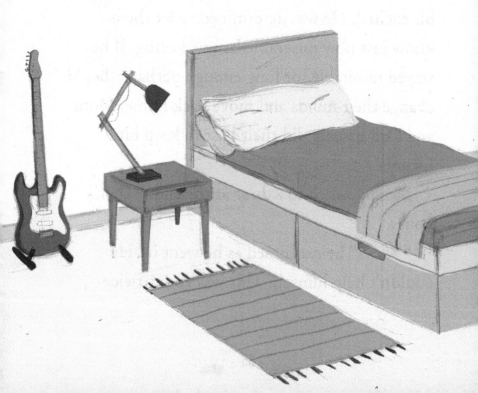

Joe tried to take everything in. This was HIS room—the place he would now sleep and chill out. It was hard not to be impressed, except that everything felt too new, too perfect. There was nothing in it that felt familiar.

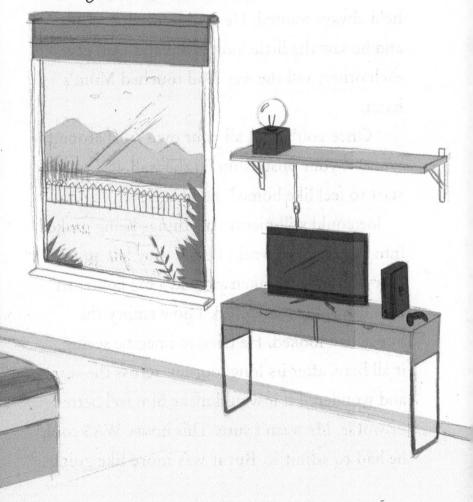

"Look, you've even got your own bathroom," said Mom, pushing open a door on the far side of the room.

Joe peered into the bathroom to the open shower, the toilet, the sink. Everything just as he'd always wanted. He couldn't help smiling and he saw the little look Mom and Dad gave each other, and the way Dad touched Mom's hand.

"Once you've got all your own stuff around you and your posters up on the wall, it'll soon start to feel like home," said Dad.

Joe could still picture his things being packed into boxes in the weeks before they left and everything being taken away in a big container on a lorry. He remembered how empty the house had looked. He tried to imagine seeing it all here, after its long journey across the sea, and wondered if it would make him feel better or worse. He wasn't sure. This house WAS cool, he had to admit it. But it was more like going-on-vacation cool. It wasn't cool like living-here-forever cool. Because this *wasn't* his cozy, lived-here-forever-smelling room at home and nothing could change that.

He made his way to the window. In the distance, jagged mountains pointed to the sky like evil fangs. Mister P. was wandering around the backyard, checking things out, sticking his head behind the backyard buildings and exploring along the fence at the back of the property, lifting himself up on his hind legs to get a better look around.

"Why do you think he's here?" Joe wondered out loud. Maybe the polar bear had abandoned the melting sea ice of the Arctic in the hope things might be better in this new place, just like Mom and Dad seemed to think things would be better. Or maybe he was as lost as Joe? Mom and Dad joined him at the window, just as Mister P. let himself out of the back gate and started trotting briskly towards the lake. They all watched as he stood like a statue at the lake's edge then suddenly pounced, scooping a paw in the water and pulling out a large fish, which he dropped into his mouth.

"I do hope he isn't going to cause trouble with the neighbors," said Mom with a sigh.

"I'd better go and make some calls right away," said Dad. "I'm sure someone will have reported a missing polar bear by now."

Joe tried to imagine who might be searching for a missing bear. Maybe they'd got Joe's luggage instead? If so, he hoped they'd look after it. He folded his arms across his chest and looked around. Not having his bag made him feel somehow unwanted—all these empty cupboards and nothing to put in them.

"Can't exactly unpack, can I?" he grumbled to Mom. She was still staring out of the window at nothing in particular—looking but not seeing. She gave a little shake as if bringing herself back to reality and ran her fingers through her hair. Her face was pale and she had dark circles under her eyes.

"We'll have to go shopping," she said. "I'll make a list. The airline has offered us some money for emergency essentials."

"Hmmm. Emergency essentials—like emergency underpants maybe?" said Joe. "With flashing blue lights?"

Mom groaned and left the room.

Joe followed, in search of the kitchen and something to drink. There were a few basics in the fridge—milk and that kind of thing. He explored the cupboards, found himself a glass, and poured himself some water.

TAP ... TAP ... TAP

A sharp black claw drummed against the glass. Joe moved over to the window and Mister P. pressed his nose against it and huffed, creating a large misty circle. Joe huffed a circle back then wrote "HELLO" across the mist. Mister P. cocked his head on one side and then the other as if trying to understand what Joe had written. In fairness, from Mister P.'s side of the glass, the word would be backwards—so even if the bear could read, it

would be pretty tricky. Joe opened the window, and leant forward, resting his chin on his hands. Mister P. rested his nose on his paws.

"So what's brought you here to this house?" asked Joe. Mister P. blinked and pushed his nose a little closer. "I'm here because of my dad. He's got the job of a lifetime—apparently—which means I get dragged along too. Have you been dragged or did you come because you wanted to?"

The bear looked at him in silence. Joe wasn't sure how easy it would be to drag a polar bear anywhere.

"Well, I guess we're both stuck here whether we like it or not. In my case, definitely NOT. I mean who'd want to live in a place like this?"

Mister P.'s nose was almost touching Joe's now and it made Joe feel very small and a little nervous. Then the bear lifted a hairy paw and rested it gently on top of Joe's hand. It was the heaviest paw Joe had ever felt. Much heavier

than Roly's paw and about a hundred times
larger. Joe placed his other hand on top of
Mister P.'s paw and Mister P. added another
paw. It turned into a silly game with each of
them taking it in turns to pull out the bottom
hand or paw and replace it on the top. Faster
and faster they went
until they couldn't
keep going any more.
Mister P. let himself
tip slowly backwards
onto the grass as if
he was exhausted.

"I used to play that game with my friends when I was younger," Joe laughed. "I haven't done it for years."

Mister P. gave a large yawn. His open mouth was almost as big as his paw and a lot more scary. Joe couldn't help yawning too. Yawns were catching like that. The bear curled himself up, closed his eyes, and started to snore. Joe

wouldn't have minded going to sleep himself, but his parents had warned him about jet lag—he needed to adjust to a new time clock and that meant trying to stay awake until *real* bed time. He looked at his watch. Proper bed time was hours away. He heard Mom come into the kitchen.

"Do you think polar bears get jet lag like we do?" Joe asked.

Mom frowned. "I don't think most polar bears spend that much time on aeroplanes."

"Agreed," said Joe, "But I don't think Mister P. is like *most* polar bears, is he?"

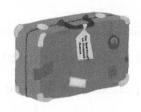

CHAPTER 4

SHOPPING AND DROPPING

Dad slammed down the telephone.

"Everyone thinks I am a hoax caller—treating me like some idiot making up a story about a polar bear coming to visit. I can't get any sense out of anyone." Dad thumped the table with his hands. "It wouldn't be like this at home. Someone would have been here right away."

"I thought you said *this* was home now," said Joe.

"Yes, well, yes it is. But . . . oh, never mind. I suppose we'll just have to hope the wretched creature goes away of his own accord."

"He's not a wretched creature," said Joe. "I like him and I don't think he has any intention of going anywhere."

Joe could see Mister P. fast asleep in the backyard, a large furry rug in the middle of the too-green grass.

"What do you call a polar bear who likes to sunbathe?" asked Joe.

Dad rolled his eyes. "I don't know," he said wearily, "what do you call a polar bear who likes to sunbathe?"

"A solar bear," said Joe and started to laugh.

Mom and Dad both moaned. "Terrible," said Mom. "Awful," said Dad.

Joe shrugged. "Just trying to cheer everyone up. So what do we do now?" he asked.

"I don't know," said Mom. "What do you feel like doing? And DON'T say "going home"," she added.

"I dunno, then," said Joe. "What *is* there to do?" Joe was used to being busy all the time.

He wasn't used to being bored. If he'd been at home—real home—he could call his friends and invite them all round to his house to play on the PlayStation or watch TV or just hang out. Or he could take Roly for a walk in the park. Roly had lots of dog friends in the park. But Joe didn't have any friends here and he didn't have Roly either. It was a confusing feeling and he didn't want to think about it too hard because it actually hurt. This must be what lonely feels like, he decided. Like a huge hurt all around you. Not that he'd ever admit to feeling miserable because Joe was always jolly—happy was pretty much his second name. Mom and Dad said that was what made him so popular, that everybody loved him because he was always so positive, but that was in his old world where he had loads of friends to cheer him along all the time. This was different.

Dad put a hand on Joe's shoulder. "The sooner you start at school, the better," said Dad, as if reading Joe's mind. "You'll soon meet lots of new people and things will seem more normal."

Joe nodded. Dad was right. He'd be fine once he got to school. Joe had been at his last school since he was five and he loved everything about it. Everybody knew him. Everybody liked him. Why should it be any different here? He'd soon have piles of friends who'd look out for him and go places with him. He tried to ignore the tiny worry worm whispering in his mind that school here might not be quite the same. He wasn't stupid. He knew going to live in another country made you an outsider and starting at a new school made you an outsider. That made him a double outsider . . . triple if you counted the wheelchair. His shoulders slumped.

"Okay, you two," said Mom. "There's no point in sitting around looking miserable. Let's go out and explore. We need to go shopping for food and some bits and pieces for Joe. If nothing else, we need to keep ourselves busy so we don't fall asleep."

"You're right." Dad was on his feet. "Come on! I was going to save this until later . . . didn't want too much excitement all at once."

"Excitement?" said Joe. "You call shopping for food and clothes *excitement*?"

Dad rubbed his hands together. "We've got a big surprise waiting for you down in the garage."

"Not another polar bear?"

Dad stuck his fingers in his ears like he always did when Joe was being silly. Then he led the way into the hall and unlocked a door that, up until this point, Joe had assumed was a closet. As the door swung open, the whole basement lit up. Another long ramp led down into a massive underground garage. And parked in the garage was the biggest, blackest, shiniest pick-up truck Joe had ever seen. The doors kind of bulged out at the sides and behind the driver and passenger cab was an open back.

"Wow! Is this ours?" Joe was impressed. It was about ten times the size of their old car at home.

"Not ours, exactly," said Dad. "The company pays for the lease. I'm going to be working in some out-of-the-way places and we're going to need something that'll cope with the road conditions you get here in the winter."

Joe made his way down to the garage to take a closer look, wondering just what kind of job Dad was going to be doing here. He ran his fingers along the glossy paintwork. Dad's engineering jobs often took him away from home, but this was the first time they'd ever had to move.

"This must have cost a fortune," Joe said, wheeling himself around the truck.

"Not our problem," said Dad. "Just need to be careful not to crash it." Dad opened the driver's door and climbed in. "OK, are you ready? Wait 'til you see this." Joe watched, astonished, as the passenger door started to open upwards like a wing on a giant blackbird. "Pretty fancy, huh?"

Joe's eyes widened. It was like something out of the movies.

"But that's not all!" continued Dad, excitedly. With a whirr and a click, a metal platform descended from the car and onto the ground.

"Wheel yourself on," said Dad.

Joe maneuvered himself onto the platform and Dad came round to secure the wheelchair in place. Then he pressed a button and Joe's platform rose up off the ground and then slid sideways into the car.

Dad had a wide smile on his face and Joe was speechless. This was way better than their car back home. This was incredible.

"You'd better not get too used to it," said Mom. "Once our five years is up, it'll be back home to the old car again."

FIVE YEARS. All Joe's excitement vanished. When Mom said it like that it sounded like a prison sentence. Joe would be sixteen by the time they went home. SIXTEEN! Could he really survive five years in this place?

"Bet you've changed your mind about shopping now," said Dad.

Joe shook away his thoughts. He most definitely hadn't changed his mind about shopping, but the car was awesome and he couldn't wait to go out for a drive.

"Can we get some photos?" said Joe. "I want to send a photo to Nico." Nico was Joe's cousin and he was a complete motor-head. He read car magazines, collected model cars, and always watched the motor racing on TV. Nico would LOVE this car.

"Let's get out into the daylight first," said Dad.

The garage door rolled open. And there, standing square in the entrance was Mister P., his nose lifting slowly upwards as he watched the door rise.

Dad shook his head. "Oh, so you're still here, are you?" he said quietly. He lowered the car window. "Go on, scoot!" he shouted. "You need to get out of the way."

Mister P. took a few steps forward and started sniffing at the front of the truck. He lifted both front paws onto the hood and then peered in the windscreen and grinned. Dad puffed out his

cheeks and then peeped the horn and revved the
engine loudly.

Mister P. jumped to one side, clearing the
way. Dad accelerated up the ramp and into the
afternoon sun. Joe kept an eye on Mister P. in
the rearview mirror. The bear chased up the
slope behind the truck and when Dad came to
a stop at the road, Mister P. climbed carefully
into the back, the truck sinking down with his
enormous weight.

Dad gripped the steering wheel and took
three big breaths as if he was trying to calm
himself. "He'd better not be scratching my

paintwork or there'll be real trouble."

"He's sitting very quietly," said Joe. "I don't think he's doing any damage."

Dad looked in the rearview mirror. "Look at the SIZE of that thing. We may not even *get* to town with him in the back."

"We won't know unless we try," said Joe. "It's a powerful truck."

"Yeah—which turns out to be lucky, under the circumstances."

"Lucky?" said Mom picking up on the end of the conversation as she climbed into the back with a large shopping bag. "What's lucky?"

Joe smiled. "Mister P. is lucky—lucky he can fit in the back of our truck."

"So we can take him to the other side of town and drop him somewhere that he'll feel more comfortable," added Dad.

"You're not going to do that, are you? You can't," cried Joe. "He's mine. I signed the papers and I think he feels perfectly comfortable here with us."

"He is *not* yours," said Dad. "You had no idea what you were signing. Honestly, we can't keep a polar bear. People will talk. And if he starts damaging our house or our car or our yard . . . I mean, he could even cost me my job!"

"Would that mean we'd have to go home?" said Joe hopefully.

Dad took three deep breaths. Mom leant forward and put her hand on Dad's shoulder. "Let's go and explore. It'll be good for us to discover more about the area. Let's not worry about Mister P. for the moment. There's a whole new world out there."

Dad wasn't used to driving such an enormous car, so no one was allowed to speak as he made his way into town. They went three times round a one-way system as they tried to find the supermarket, then Dad had to stop the car while he and Mom had an argument. Mister P. sat tall in the back of the truck, surveying his surroundings. Finally they spotted the entrance to the supermarket and Dad dropped Mom and Joe right outside and went off to park.

Mom dragged Joe around the huge store for what seemed like hours, picking up what she called "essential" items of clothing and food. Dad didn't reappear.

By the time they'd paid for everything and got out of the supermarket, Dad was waiting right where he'd dropped them earlier. But there was NO MISTER P.

Joe was angry. Really angry. "What have you done with him?" he demanded.

"Dropped him somewhere where he'll be

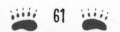

much happier," said Dad.

"Well I'm not getting back in this car until you tell me where he is."

"Joe, he's a wild animal. He doesn't belong in our house. It's not what he's used to."

"It's not what I'm used to either," Joe said, giving his dad his best drop-dead look.

Dad sighed. "Don't make this harder than it already is. Get in the car."

Joe closed his eyes for a moment and tried to shut out everything that was happening. Then he manoeuvred himself into the car. "Mister P. will be back," he said. "We've still got his suitcase. And how many wild animals do you know with a suitcase?"

Dad face-planted onto the steering wheel, making the horn peep loudly so that everyone looked at them. Mom and Joe glanced at each other and then laughed.

"Okay, o . . . kay," said Dad. "Here's the deal. If that bear comes back for his suitcase, then I promise I'll let him stay."

CHAPTER 5
NEWS AND VIEWS

That evening, the dark crept in early. Mister P. hadn't returned and his suitcase sat in the corner of Joe's room. Joe stared sadly at the blank screen of his computer. He had promised to email his friends and tell them **everything**. He knew there was plenty to write about, but he couldn't find the enthusiasm to write a single word. All his friends back at home had been in a whirlwind of excitement about Joe's big move. Everyone said Joe was so lucky and they wished they could swap places with him. Even Joe had been excited at first—about the idea of it, at least. He'd talked it up a lot—made it sound like the best thing ever—so now that he was actually here, he'd have to live up to everyone's expectations. He looked around at his perfect room, his new games console, his guitar. People would kill for this kind of house. He had everything he could possibly want. He knew he was lucky, but the trouble was . . . it wasn't things that really mattered. It was people—friends. And Joe knew he mustn't let down his friends by sounding sad and homesick. That wasn't what they wanted to hear.

Joe's eyelids started to droop. The jet lag was kicking in and he had to shake himself awake and try to force his eyes to stay open. He calculated the time difference and was envious that all his friends would be fast asleep in their beds. It was a weird feeling. Joe wondered if his new bed would be as comfortable as his one at home. He gave an enormous stretch then forced himself to turn on his laptop and check his emails.

Noah was Joe's oldest friend. They had
been born on the same day in the same
hospital, but Joe was older by four hours
and twenty-six minutes. Noah's dad was a
musician and he'd been teaching Joe guitar
for nearly three years. Noah played drums.
They lived—used to live, Joe corrected
himself—on the next street, and Noah's
dad had a music studio in the garage. Noah
and Joe spent hours and hours and hours
together practising and hanging out in that
garage. How could he ever replace a friend
like that?

Joe sighed and pressed reply. He
decided he must sound happy whatever.

Hi Noah

It is all good here. Our house is pretty nice and my bedroom is great. We have a huge garage. Your dad would love it. Will send photos soon.

It's a weird place and the people are a bit strange. Not that I've met very many yet. My suitcase went missing at the airport, but a polar bear turned up instead. I'm not even joking. Dad said he couldn't stay and has sent him off into the wild, but I'm really hoping he'll come back because he is quite cool.

It's not the same without you guys around but I guess I'll get used to it.

If you see Roly, give him a hug from me.

Joe

Joe re-read his message a few times and pressed **send.** He wished Noah were there. He wished Roly were there. Mom came in with a steaming mug of hot chocolate. "Dad's lit the fire. Why don't you come and join us in the living room instead of sitting in here by yourself? It's very warm and cozy. We could play a game if you like."

Joe yawned and stretched again. His brain was fuzzy and his eyes hurt. He took a sip of chocolate. "I'm so tired, Mom. I feel like my head is about to fall off my shoulders."

"That would be disappointing," said Mom.

"I suppose it would mean I could see under the bed more easily," said Joe, doing his best to be his normal jokey self.

Mom smiled and went to pull the curtains closed.

"Don't," said Joe. "I'd rather leave them open." It was a clear night with a full moon and Joe remembered Gran telling him that the same moon would shine on both of them, however far apart they were. Somehow shutting out the moon felt like shutting in the loneliness.

"Have you tried your guitar yet?" Mom asked. "A practice session might wake you up a bit."

"What's the point?" Joe shrugged. "I've got no one to practise with and nothing to practise for." Last year, Noah and Joe had invited Ellie and Kasia to join their band. Kasia was quite good at the keyboard and Ellie could sing really well. This year their band had won at the finals of the local schools' competition and everyone at school thought they were legends. One girl had even asked Joe for his autograph, which was funny. Now all those good memories seemed like sad memories and he didn't want to look at his guitar or think about music. He lowered his eyes to the floor.

"Hey, where's happy Joe gone?" said Mom.

Joe tried to squeeze a smile onto his face.

"You've done really well getting through today," she said. "I know it's hard, but if you can manage to stay awake for another hour or so, it'll help you get your new time clock sorted out."

Joe wanted to tell Mom that he wasn't interested in a new time clock. And if she thought he was doing really well, she was wrong. Inside he was doing really, miserably badly. He moved to the window so that Mom wouldn't see the tears glistening in the corners of his eyes. The moon floated pale and ghostly on the lake. And something cast a shadow. A big bear-shaped shadow!

Joe blinked and shook his head in case he was imagining things. It was Mister P.—he was sure!

"He's back," he whispered. "Mom, look! Mister P. is back."

Mom joined him at the window. She and Joe bumped fists. It was what they always did when things were good.

"I knew he'd be back," said Joe. "I knew Dad was wrong. Mister P. wants to be here with us, he doesn't want to be anywhere else." He watched the bear walking slowly around the lake. Seeing Mister P. again made Joe want to laugh out loud.

"Do you think polar bears get lonely living by themselves all the time?"

"I don't know," said Mom. "I think they are quite solitary creatures."

"Unlike humans."

"Some humans are solitary," said Mom.

"Not me," said Joe.

"No, not you." Mom smiled and ruffled his hair.

Joe ducked his head out of the way. "Stop doing that, will you? You know I hate it."

"Just making sure your head is still attached to your shoulders. You'd better come and give Dad the news. He'll have to stick to his word about letting Mister P. stay. He promised."

At that moment the polar bear looked up from what he was doing and stared up at the sky. He looked so beautiful standing out there silhouetted against the moon and it made a shiver go down Joe's back. Did the moon look the same wherever you were in the world, Joe wondered. Would his friends look at the moon and think about him? He hoped so.

In the living room, the warm orange glow from the fire was a sharp contrast to the pale cold outside. He managed two games of Racing Demon before his eyes closed and, however hard he tried, they would not open again. He didn't remember being put to bed.

That night, he dreamed he was playing with the band, then woke in a strange and unfamiliar darkness and couldn't work out where he was. He fumbled for a light switch. Light flooded the room and he stared around him, trying to make sense of his surroundings.

And slowly he remembered. This was his new world.

CHAPTER 6
TIPS AND TRIPS

Joe must have slept again because he woke to the sound of a massive noise and kerfuffle going on outside. First there was the unmistakable sound of a lawnmower. This in itself was not surprising. Dad was obsessive about mowing the lawn into neat stripes. But there was something else. Joe sat up and rubbed his eyes. Every few seconds he saw a frantic furball racing past the window at top speed. It was Mister P. and he looked absolutely terrified. Perhaps Mister P. thought Dad was going to mow his fur into neat stripes too!

The thought of a stripy polar bear made Joe giggle, but only for a moment. Joe started to worry that Dad may scare Mister P. so badly that the bear would run away.

"Morning," said Mom, putting her head round the door. "How did you sleep?"

"On and off," said Joe.

"Me too." The sight of Mister P. hurtling past made Mom hurry to the window. She covered her mouth with her hand as she tried to stifle a laugh.

"It's not funny," said Joe. "Look at the poor animal. He's scared half to death. I doubt he's ever seen a lawnmower before. Tell Dad to stop."

"Tell your father to stop mowing the lawn? You have to be kidding me."

Joe knew Mom was right. "In that case," he said, "just help me out of bed quickly so I can go and rescue Mister P."

"Fine," said Mom. "But do not let him in the house or Dad will have a fit."

As soon as Joe was in his chair, he headed straight out of his room and toward the back door. He put two fingers in his mouth and gave a loud whistle that cut through the sound of the

mower. Mister P. stopped in his tracks and turned. When he saw Joe, he galloped towards him at high speed, almost landing in Joe's lap. He flung his front legs round Joe's neck and clung on so tight that Joe could hardly breathe, let alone speak.

"Hello Mister P., welcome back," said Joe with his mouth half stuffed with polar bear fur. Joe stroked the bear gently and tried to calm him down. The poor animal was shaking from head to toe. Joe would *have* to bring him inside. What else could he do?

He reversed a little and Mister P. loosened his grip. "Come with me," Joe whispered, "It's safe inside, as long as you stay very quiet so no one knows you are here."

Joe checked to make sure Mom wasn't watching then led Mister P. along the corridor and into his bedroom. As the lawnmower approached the window, Mister P. flattened himself on the floor next to the bed, pulling Joe's covers over the top of himself. He lay absolutely still.

"Welcome to my room," said Joe, "make yourself at home, why don't you?"

Mister P. pressed the covers against his ears with his paws.

"Don't worry, Dad will be finished soon."

Dad continued up and down and up and down until the rough green grass was manicured into perfect light and dark stripes. It looked strange and out of place with the wilderness of the lake and mountains beyond. Joe listened as the sound of the mower dwindled away.

"You can come out now," Joe whispered to Mister P. "The mowing's all done. We'd better get you back outside before anyone finds you."

But Mister P. refused to budge. Joe understood how he felt—he understood what it was like to want to hide from things that frightened you. He also knew hiding wasn't the answer. He lifted the covers very slightly. "Hey, come on! You'll soon get used to the mower. Trust me, it won't seem half as scary next time round."

Mister P. pulled the covers back over his head. Joe tried to think of a way to tempt Mister P. out. He searched around the room and spotted Mister P.'s suitcase. He picked it up and placed it in front of Mister P.'s nose.

"What have you got in here?" asked Joe lifting the covers away from Mister P.'s eyes.

At the sight of the suitcase, Mister P. started to edge his way forward. Using the very tips of his claws, Mister P. carefully undid the catches and opened the lid. Joe peered in at the strange assortment of objects: a soccer ball, some headphones, a cap, a harmonica, and a toy monkey.

"Are these all yours, Mister P.?" he asked.

Mister P. touched each one gently with his paw then grabbed the headphones and put them over his ears.

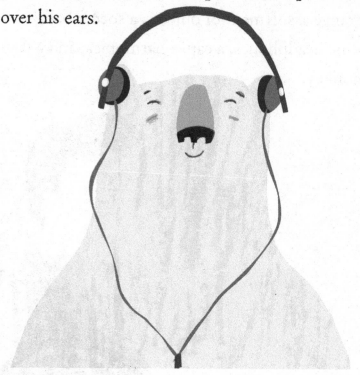

Joe wasn't sure what he'd expected to find in a polar bear's suitcase. He leant forward to take a closer look, but Mister P. snapped the suitcase shut and put his head back under the covers.

BING BONG BING BONG BING BONG

A horrible tinny noise sung through the house. Joe decided it could only be the doorbell. He hoped it wasn't the neighbors complaining about Mister P. catching fish in the lake or charging up and down the lawn.

BING BONG BING BONG BING BONG

Joe waited for Mom to answer the door. He moved closer to his bedroom door so he could hear. "Hello . . . welcome . . . nice to meet you." Chitter chatter, chitter chatter.

"Joe," called Mom. "Jo-oe." Mom had a clever way of making his name into two syllables when she was calling him. "We have visitors." He heard Mom's footsteps coming along the corridor.

"Uh-oh," said Joe. "Here comes trouble."

"Joe!" called Mom again, pushing open the door before Joe had time to block her entrance.

"Good grief!" Mom walked into the room and stopped. "What is that bear doing under your covers?"

"Hiding," said Joe. There wasn't much point in lying.

"Hiding from what?"

Joe shrugged. "Visitors he doesn't want to see?"

"Visitors *you* don't want to see, more like. I told you not to let that bear in the house. And how do you know you don't want to see them, you don't even know who they are." Mom hissed all this in a grumpy whisper.

"So who *are* they?" Joe hissed back.

"One of Dad's new work colleagues and his son who is the same age as you and will be in your year at school. They're waiting to meet you." Mister P. peeked out from under the covers.

"And what is he doing wearing your headphones?"

"They're not mine," said Joe. "They're his."

Mom removed the headphones, inspected them, and put them on the side. "Right, Mister P.," she said. "You stay here. I'll be back to deal with you later."

Joe pulled an apologetic face at Mister P. and followed Mom out of the door. As he approached the kitchen he heard the man's voice. "And we wondered if Joe enjoys ice hockey. We have four teams in school, don't we, Austin? I'm the head coach, as it happens. It's a great way to get to know people and have fun."

Joe slowed for a moment, glanced at Mom, and then went full speed ahead, almost skidding into the kitchen.

"Not sure I'll be much help on your ice hockey team," he said, a little too aggressively. "Hi, I'm Joe. Nice to meet you." He waited for one of them to stick out an arm to shake hands.

He saw the boy look at him—well, at his chair—and then look at the ground. Disappointment. Embarrassment. That was the look. Joe had seen it before but usually he had friends to back him up. Not here.

Joe held out his hand to the man who was tall and kind of beefy-looking with a bald head.

The man pumped Joe's arm up and down, nearly crushing his hand. "Hi there. Good to meet you. I'm Simon Wildman. And this is my boy, Austin.'

Mr. Wildman gave Austin a small shove and Austin stepped forward. He had

straight fair hair and freckles and looked
nothing like his dad. Austin raised a hand and
said, "Hi," in a shy kind of way.

"We've brought a welcome gift for you," said
Mr. Wiseman. "Haven't we, Austin?"

Austin fumbled in his pocket and pulled out an envelope. From the look on his face, Austin didn't seem too certain about handing it over.

Admit one Ice-hockey ...rday

Admit one Ice-hockey Saturday

"Tickets to the ice hockey game at the weekend," said Mr. Wildman. "It's a big game this Saturday. Austin's older brother plays for the local team—and Austin will too, one day." A huge look of pride was planted on Mr. Wildman's face as he looked at his son. Austin didn't look so sure.

"Do you like ice hockey?" asked Austin.

"It's not really that big where we come from," Joe said, thinking that watching ice hockey might be about as exciting as watching slugs racing.

Mr. Wildman rolled his eyes. "Well, it's barely worth living round here if you don't support the local team."

"I'm sure we'll enjoy supporting the local team," said Dad, smiling. "Won't we, Joe?"

Joe looked at his Dad in disbelief. Dad was even less keen on sport than he was.

"Joe's more into music than sport really," said Mom in a soothing voice. Joe wanted to drop through the floorboards. He guessed that the mention of a word like *music* would be enough to make people like the Wildmans snore with boredom. Why couldn't Mom keep her mouth shut?

To Joe's surprise, Austin grinned. "I like music too. I play the ukulele at school. I'm not much good at it, but we had to choose an instrument to learn so that's what I chose."

Mr. Wildman roared with laughter and waved Austin's words away, as if learning the ukulele was about the silliest thing he'd ever heard. Austin shuffled his feet and looked at the ground. "The thing is," said Mr. Wildman, sounding serious. "If you really want to fit in around here, then the ice hockey stadium is the place to be!"

"But Joe won't be able to sit with us," said Austin, looking at Joe's chair.

"That doesn't matter," said Mr. Wildman. "It's the game that matters. And there's no problem with wheelchairs . . . none at all. Brand new stadium. All kitted out."

Joe decided he would be the judge of that. Just because a place advertised itself as wheelchair-friendly, it didn't always mean it was so friendly for the person *in* the wheelchair. Not being able to sit with friends wasn't Joe's definition of friendly for a start. Back at home, everyone would have come and sat with him.

"So, are you up for it?" Mr. Wildman took the tickets from Austin and held them out to Dad. "We've got you four tickets and some supporters" kit too—hats, foam fingers, that kind of thing. It'll help you feel at home in the crowd and we wouldn't want you mistakenly supporting the wrong team.' He laughed as he passed over a large bag. "When you've been to one game you'll be hooked, I guarantee."

"We only need three tickets," said Mom. "It's just the three of us."

"Four," said Joe. "Mister P. will definitely want to come. Ice hockey will be right up his street."

"Mister P.?" said Mr. Wildman.

"My polar bear," said Joe, glancing at Dad. Dad narrowed his eyes in a warning kind of way.

Mr. Wildman shook his head. "You don't need a ticket for a cuddly toy. You can just bring the bear along, no problem. Don't worry about the spare ticket, Austin's got tons of friends who'd like to come."

Tons of friends. Each word hit Joe like a thump in the chest and it made him angry. In fact Mr. Wildman was starting to wind him up.

"Actually, Mister P. is not a cuddly toy. He's a real polar bear." Joe kept his voice very calm.

"And I'd like to bring him because he can come and sit with me and keep me company, seeing as Austin and all his friends won't be able to."

There was an awkward silence. Joe was amused to see his parents looking utterly helpless. He put two fingers in his mouth and whistled loudly. From the direction of his bedroom came the unmistakable

thud, thud, thud

of polar bear paws and a few moments later Mister P. stuck his head round the kitchen door and stood blinking at the assembled group.

"So . . ." said Joe, the smallest hint of triumph in his voice as he looked at Mr. Wildman's shocked face, ". . . *this* is Mister P.".

Austin took one step sideways so he was more or less hidden behind his dad, who took one step backwards at the same time and ended up stamping on Austin's foot.

Mister P. stood up on his hind legs, his great furry head brushing the high ceiling. At full height, he made Mr. Wildman look small. Mr. Wildman's eyes rose up and up and the look on his face was brilliant. Mister P. stuck out a large, hairy paw. Joe waited to see what would happen next.

Slowly and carefully, Mr. Wildman held out a thick arm towards the bear, gripped Mister P.'s paw, and started to pump it up and down. Mister P. seemed to think this was some kind of game and wouldn't let go. Small beads of sweat formed on Mr. Wildman's forehead. Joe's sides nearly split as he tried to hold back his laughter.

"Good to meet you, Mister P.," said Mr. Wildman in a rather high voice. Mister P. grinned a huge grin. Up and down, up and down went Mr. Wildman's arm. Finally the bear let go and Mr. Wildman's arm flopped loosely by his side.

Joe watched to see what Austin would do. Austin looked Joe right in the eye. He stepped out from behind his dad and stuck out his skinny arm to shake Mister P.'s paw. He gave one gentle shake, took the spare ticket from his dad, and handed it to Joe.

"Bring the bear," he said. "It'd be cool."

"Great," said Joe. "We'll see you on Saturday, then." Mister P. already had his nose in the plastic bag of supporters' kit and was spreading items around the kitchen.

Mr. Wildman mopped his head with a large spotted handkerchief and looked at his watch. "We'd better be off. We have ice hockey training this evening. We'll catch you at the game." He frowned at Mister P. "I hope you can keep that creature of yours under control."

"Oh he's fine . . . most of the time," said Joe. "As long as you don't annoy him."

Mr. Wildman edged his way past the bear and towards the front door. Austin gave Mister P. a friendly stroke as he passed.

Mom, Dad, Joe, and Mister P. watched as the Wildmans drove away down Pinewood Avenue.

"Well, they were nice," said Mom, in her jolliest voice.

Joe raised his eyes to the ceiling.

"Well they *were*," said Mom emphatically. "And it was very kind of them to give us those tickets. I'm sure you and Austin . . ."

"Oh, come on, Mom. He plays the ukulele and ice hockey. And he hardly says a word. Me and Austin are about as likely to be friends as a hungry polar bear and a seal."

Mister P. hung his head and gave a low growl.

"What?" said Joe, looking at the bear.

Mom put her hand on Mister P.'s back. "I agree with the bear," she said. "Don't judge people too quickly. First impressions are often wrong."

"Since when did you speak polar bear," said Joe. He wasn't in the mood to be lectured. He went back to his room, slammed the door, and switched on his laptop. He needed some real friend time.

CHAPTER 7
PLAYING AND PAYING

To: Joe

From: Ellie

Q: What do I call our school now you've left?

A: A no-Joe area (haha—do you get it? Like no-go area, except . . . well you know!). In fact maybe that should be a no-joke area. Honestly, I haven't laughed once since you left.

It was impossible to picture Ellie not laughing. When she and Joe got going with the jokes, they laughed until every muscle in their stomachs ached. Joe couldn't imagine ever laughing like that again. He'd only known her for three years, but she was one of those people who made everything fun. And she always stuck up for him and made sure he was OK getting on and off the bus. He carried on reading.

Seriously, school is really dull without you. Mr. Pritchard says we might actually get some work done for a change! I don't think he means it because he keeps looking at where you used to sit and making a sad face. Have you started at your new school yet? Met anyone nice?

Noah said to ask you if the polar bear came back. I presume the bear is a joke?

Ellie X

To: Ellie
From: Joe

First up, the polar bear is back and it's not a joke (see attached photo).

I've only met one person so far and his name is Austin Wildman. WILDMAN?! Can you believe that name? I mean he was OK—about as wild as a very tame poodle and not exactly a bundle of laughs so I'm not sure we'll ever be best friends. His dad is quite scary, though. I don't think I made a very good first impression because I don't know anything about ice hockey and EVERYONE round here is an ice hockey fanatic (according to Mr. Wildman at least). So it looks like I'm going to fit in really well (NOT).

School starts next week.

I'll keep you posted.

Joe.

A message pinged straight back.

From Ellie: Ice hockey is FUN. You should go and watch a game. Ellie X

From Joe: You'd better be right. I'm going to watch a game tomorrow.

From Ellie: Have AN ICE time. Hahahaha.
D'you get it? Have a nice time.
From Joe: Stop explaining your jokes. Of course I
get it. I'm not dumb.
From Ellie: Sorreeeee.

Joe decided he really, really, really missed Ellie. Or perhaps he just missed laughing.

From Ellie: Check out this link.

Joe pressed on the link. Up came a load of information about ice hockey. That was typical Ellie. She was always right on to everything. If Joe was ever worried about doing something, she'd be straight off to find out all the information. Her conclusion was always the same, *If you don't try, you'll never know,* which meant Joe felt he had to give everything a go, just to stop her nagging. Sometimes it was annoying, but she made him do things that he'd never have thought about if she hadn't been there. He could do with Ellie around now. He started to scan the info when another email pinged through.

From Ellie: Did Noah tell you that Suzy is taking your place in the band? I'm not that thrilled, to be honest, but we had to find someone. It won't be the same.

Joe pushed himself away from the computer so he couldn't see the screen. Suzy had been trying to muscle in on the band for months. She fancied herself as a really good guitar player, though she hadn't been playing for nearly as long as Joe. Worse still, she was incredibly bossy. How dare the others let her take his place in the band? No one could take his place. It would be a disaster.

As if to prove this to himself, he picked up his new guitar and plugged in the amp. He started to pick at the strings and to strum a few chords. Within about thirty seconds, Mister P.'s head appeared round the door. He padded cautiously into the room and pressed his nose right into Joe's guitar strings. The amplifier rumbled and then squealed and Mister P. spun round and crouched in front of the speaker, growling at it, ready to pounce.

"Leave it," said Joe. "Come away from there." He started to play again and soon Mister P. began to sway to the beat. Joe turned up the volume and Mister P. swayed a little more.

"OK, Mister Disco Bear," he said laughing, "wait until you see this!" Joe flicked the switch on his disco ball and his bedroom burst into colour that swirled and twirled in Mister P.'s shiny black eyes and reflected off his fur like tiny rainbows. Music vibrated through the whole house and, before long, Mister P. and Joe were rocking round the room for all they were worth.

Joe had forgotten what this felt like. It was *brilliant*. So brilliant, in fact, that he didn't even see Dad storm in—not until Dad had cut the switch to the amplifier, filling the room with a big, fat

SILENCE.

Joe stopped playing and Mister P. came to a stop, breathing heavily.

"For goodness" sake, what's got into you?' cried Dad. "I've already had next door coming round to complain. Apparently there's rules about this kind of thing round here."

The big balloon of happiness inside Joe deflated to nothing. Mister P. looked solemnly at Dad and then at Joe.

"It's not my fault," said Joe. "Mister P. wanted to join in. We were having fun!"

Dad's face softened. "Yeah, well unfortunately our neighbors don't want to join in. And they *weren't* having fun! In fairness, Joe, it was quite LOUD."

"No one used to complain at home."

"That's probably because Noah's garage was professionally soundproofed, thanks to his dad."

"Well, you'll have to soundproof our garage then," Joe demanded, throwing his guitar back onto its stand and turning off the disco lights.

"And who's going to pay for *that*, then? You've got all this new kit. Isn't that enough?" said Dad, his voice starting to rise again.

"NO! It's not!"

"Joe," said Dad, "What is the matter with you?"

"Suzy's taken my place in the band." The words tumbled out of Joe's mouth without him thinking about it.

"Ah," said Dad, realization dawning on his face. "So that's what this is *really* about. You should be pleased they're keeping going. Would you want to see the band fall apart, just because you've left?"

"Yes."

"What about Noah and Ellie and Kasia?" asked Dad. "It wouldn't be very fair on them, would it? Life can't stop just because you're not there any more. Who knows, you might set up a new band here."

"I won't. It wouldn't be the same."

"Of course it wouldn't. Life can't always stay the same. We have to adjust to new situations and make the most of them. The world doesn't revolve around Joe Beechcroft. We have to move on."

"We didn't *have* to move on," said Joe. "You *decided* to move on."

Mister P. gave a huge yawn and sat down next to Dad.

"And since when did Mister P. think it was OK to live in your room?" asked Dad. "I suppose that was *your* decision?"

Mister P. was shifting from paw to paw as he listened to them arguing.

"No, it was his. I suppose *he* decided to make

the most of *his* new situation."

"Fair answer," said Dad, his face suddenly relaxing into a smile. "Right, I'll leave you to it then. I've got work to do. But if you want to practise your guitar, please keep the volume down. We don't want to make enemies of our neighbors."

Once Dad had gone, Joe sat in silence for a while, trying to make sense of his feelings. He wasn't used to Dad arguing with him. He was used to getting his own way. He *liked* getting his own way. If he wanted to play music loudly, he'd play music loudly. If he didn't want to go to an ice hockey game, then he wouldn't go. But in this new world, things seemed to work differently.

"The thing is, Mister P.," Joe said miserably. "I set up that band with Noah. It was OUR thing. Someone can't just come in and take my place. Why should Suzy get to have all the fun when I'm stuck here with no one? How is that fair on me?"

Mister P. rested his chin on Joe's lap and looked up at him.

"I don't suppose you'd understand. You're only a polar bear. I bet you don't even know what a band is."

Mister P. sighed and let his head drop to the floor.

CHAPTER 8
CROWDS AND CLOUDS

To: Joe

From: Nico

How's it going dude? Thanks for the photo of your new car. JEALOUS! Mom says that it will only take me a thousand car washes to earn enough to come and visit you. Today I've washed Dad's car, Gran's car, and my brother's van. Three down, 997 to go! I'll see you in about ten years!

Nico

It was the morning of the ice hockey game. Joe hadn't seen Mister P. since breakfast and he'd kept himself occupied playing games on his

computer. Seeing Nico's message was good—
and bad. Nico's car washing was legendary.
He was always washing cars to get money for
something. Sometimes he did it for charity.
Once he did it to raise money so he could go on
school camp. Usually he was saving up to buy a
new computer game, which he'd play for weeks
before challenging Joe. Nico liked to win. So did
Joe. Mom and Aunty Julie said Joe's room was
more like a war zone than a bedroom when he
and Nico were battling it out for top position.
He'd give anything to find another 997 cars for
Nico to wash. The thought of having Nico here
was brilliant—the chance of him ever earning
enough money to get here was ZERO.

He looked at his watch. It wasn't time to
get ready for the ice hockey yet. He put on his
headphones and went back to his game . . . until
suddenly his world turned black! Something
soft and spongy was covering his eyes. From
the fishy smell, Joe decided whatever it was

had something do with Mister P., though it certainly didn't feel like a polar bear paw. The pressure on his eyes released and he spun round and came face to face with a sight he never thought he'd *ever* see! Mister P. was wearing a woolly hat and had a giant foam glove on each paw. Upon each pointy finger was written The Belton Bears. Mister P. danced around raising one paw into the air and then the other.

"Mom! Dad!" laughed Joe. "Come and get this crazy bear out of my bedroom before he does some serious damage."

Mom and Dad appeared, also wearing bobble hats and giant gloves.

Joe face-planted on to his desk. "What are you all doing?" he groaned.

"Getting ready for the big game, of course," said Dad.

Mom held out a bobble hat and foam glove to Joe. "Here you go. Here's your kit. And— *look!*—the emblem for **The Belton Bears** looks like Mister P. It must be fate."

Mom and Dad held up their foam gloves next to Mister P.'s face. Joe had to admit that the emblem did look a little bit like Mister P., but that was hardly surprising given the team's name.

"What if I decide I don't want to support the Belton Bears? What if I prefer the other team?"

"Don't be deliberately difficult," said Dad. "The Belton Bears are our *home* team now. Why would you support another team?"

Joe shrugged and chucked his kit onto the bed. "We never supported our local soccer ball team at home."

"Ice hockey is a big part of this place. We need to show willing and get involved," said Mom. "It's all part of fitting in. I'm quite excited."

If Joe was really honest with himself, he was quite excited too, but he wasn't going to admit it.

And as for Mister P. . . . he just thought his foam gloves were the coolest thing on the planet.

* * *

Mister P. caused quite a stir on the way to the stadium. Lots of loyal supporters beeped their horns and waved as they went past. Mister P. pointed his foam finger at the sky and waved at all the passers-by.

"This is great," enthused Dad. "I'm loving it already."

Mom had been on the phone to the stadium to check for wheelchair access and, for once, everything went smoothly—well, in terms of the practical stuff anyway. As soon as they were out of the truck, Joe had to admit that the sense of excitement was infectious. The crowd was buzzing and the atmosphere was electric.

Mister P. was an instant celebrity and was milking it for all he was worth. He posed with fellow ice hockey supporters and high-fived anyone who approached him. It reminded Joe of all the attention he used to get when their band played, when people wanted photos taken with him, and he couldn't help feeling a twinge of jealousy.

"Come ON, Mister P.,"
said Joe grumpily, "or the
game will be over before
we've found our seats."

When they showed
their entrance tickets, the
officials were a bit awkward about the bear, but
Dad mentioned Simon Wildman's name which
seemed to make everything all right. Mister P.
stayed close to Joe and swaggered his way into
the stadium. People were milling around in
groups, heading for their various seats around
the stadium. Joe and his parents were directed to
the wheelchair-accessible area. This was the bit
Joe dreaded . . . the bit where he felt singled out
and noticed for the wrong reasons. Everyone
else of his age seemed to be with a bunch of
friends and Joe knew, if he'd been with his own
friends, they would have stuck with him and
made him feel like he belonged. Today he felt
self-conscious and alone in the crowd. If Ellie

Admit one
Ice-hockey
Saturday

Admit one
Ice-hockey
Saturday

had been here, she would have punched him on the shoulder and told him to "get over himself". But, then again, if Ellie had been here, she would have been standing beside him with Noah and Nico and a load of others. He punched himself on the shoulder, spun around in a circle, and forced a smile. At least he'd got Mister P., and not many people could boast a polar bear as a companion.

Joe ended up in a pretty prime position. He had a good view of the whole stadium and it was filling up fast. He had never visited an ice

rink before—and nor had Mister P., by the looks of things. Separating the ice from the seated area was a low solid barrier topped by see-through Perspex panels. Mister P. sat with his nose pressed hard against the Perspex, between his two glove-covered paws. The players weren't on the ice yet but there was still lots going on. Every now and again, Mister P. would sniff and scratch away at the bottom of the barrier as if he was trying to find a way to get through and onto the ice. Joe hoped the barrier was strong.

Over the other side of the arena, settled in a long line of blue plastic seats, Joe spotted Austin. Well, more specifically, he spotted Mr. Wildman (because Mr. Wildman, being so tall, was not difficult to spot) and after that he saw Austin, who was mucking around with a big group of friends, laughing and joking. This Austin looked very different from the quiet, shy person Joe had met in his kitchen. Suddenly Austin raised his hand and waved and Joe could see him chatting to his friends, pointing in Joe's direction. Joe's face flushed hot and he looked at the ground. He didn't want to be pointed at or pointed out. He took a deep breath and looked back up. Austin waved again. Joe was about to raise his own hand when Mister P. stood up on his hind legs and waved both paws high in the air.

All Austin's friends stood up and waved back which seemed to set some giant Mexican Wave in motion that went the whole way round the arena. All the fans, regardless of which team they were supporting, were swept up in a sense of shared fun and friendliness. Joe joined in, raising his hands and cheering each time the wave reached his section. Every time the wave reached Joe and Mister P., the cheers became deafening. Mister P. was clearly having the time of his life.

The music started and an enthusiastic voice came over the loudspeakers.

ARE YOU READY...

...TO...

...RUMMMMMMMMBLE?

At the sound of the loud voice echoing around the stadium, Mister P. looked a little nervous, but as soon as the music started again, he was back up on his hind legs pumping his gloved paws up and down in time to the beat. "Sit down, sit down," shouted the people behind. "We can't see. You're too big."

Joe pulled Mister P. back down into the sitting position but as the players skated onto the ice, Mister P. couldn't control himself and was up again, his front paws resting on top of the Perspex barrier, his long snout tipped over the edge.

"Get down, you daft bear," said Joe and apologized to the people behind. Mister P. slid back down and kept himself nice and low, his head zipping from left to right as he tried to keep up with the action. Suddenly a group of five players hurtled straight towards them and slammed against the barrier with an almighty

Joe and Mister P. looked at each other, wide-eyed and open-mouthed. Down here, next to the ice, every crash, bang, and thud vibrated through their bones and the speed of the skaters was breathtaking.

It was easy to identify Austin's brother as his name, **WILDMAN**, was written in large red letters across his shirt. The trouble was, **WILDMAN** wasn't playing very well and the Belton Bears weren't winning. Joe didn't understand the rules, except that it was obvious when one team or the other scored a goal . . . and Austin's brother had already missed three.

At the end of the first twenty minutes there was a break. Joe felt a tap on his shoulder and turned to see Austin behind him. "Hot chocolate!" he announced handing over two large paper cups. "One for you and one for Mister P. Are you enjoying the game? I wish I was down here with you guys. My brother's playing really badly and Dad's having a meltdown. I have to get back to my seat, but I'll catch you later."

Joe barely had time to say thank you before Austin raced off. He smiled as he held the hot chocolate. It was nice of Austin to come down. He'd have liked him to stay. He held out the steaming cup of chocolate to Mister P. The bear curled his tongue into it and took a slurp, making a funny sound as the hot liquid hit his tongue.

"THLUB-A-LUB-A-LUB-LUBBER," Mister P. half lapped and half chomped at the cup, tipping it right up and spilling pale brown liquid all over the place. *"THLUB-A-LUB-A-LUB-A-LUBBER."* Joe laughed.

Once Mister P. had finished splattering the floor with his drink, Joe sipped at his own chocolate, letting the heat warm him from the inside. He glanced up at Mr. Wildman, who was flinging his arms around as he talked to the person next to him. Joe didn't quite know what to make of Austin. Maybe his first impressions had been wrong.

The next session of the game went better for the Belton Bears and Joe found himself getting a bit more into it. When the Belton Bears took the lead he saw Mr. Wildman pumping the air with his fists and the stadium filled with foam fingers pointing towards the roof. The arena got noisier and noisier and, with an over-enthusiastic polar bear sitting beside him, it was hard for Joe not to enjoy it. At the end of the third session, as the final whistle went, the Belton Bears had won, five goals to three and the arena went wild.

On the way out, Joe saw Mr. Wildman striding towards them. "Great result," he shouted, his voice hoarse from so much cheering. "If you bring us luck like that, we need the Beechcrofts and their bear at EVERY game!"

Mom beamed and Dad gave Mr. Wildman a very un-Dad-like high five.

"Told you you'd be hooked," croaked Mr. Wildman. "I'll get you tickets for the next game."

Austin jogged up to join his dad. He must have said goodbye to all his friends as he was on his own now.

"Mister P. is a legend!" Austin exclaimed. "The star of the show. All my friends want to meet him now. Did you see him joining in and everything? He was like the biggest fan ever. I couldn't stop laughing. He was SO cool." Austin was breathless with excitement.

Joe felt another sharp stab of jealousy. So all Austin's friends wanted to meet Mister P., did they? No mention of them wanting to meet Joe. He moved quickly towards the car and came to a halt. He was gutted—everything was about Mister P.

Dad pressed the key fob and the car door opened.

"Wow," said Austin with a big smile on his face. "That's impressive."

"Yep," said Joe sounding as unimpressed as it was possible to sound.

Austin shrugged and his smile vanished. "I guess I'll see you around then," he said.

"I guess so," replied Joe. The words came out flat and dull.

"Goodbye, Mister P. Good work." Austin gave Mister P. a high five and watched him jump into the back of the truck.

"For goodness" sake, Joe,' said Dad as they lined up to get out of the car park, "you could try to sound a little more enthusiastic. Poor Austin was trying to be nice to you and all he got was some kind of grunt and mumble."

"Poor Austin? What d'you mean, poor Austin? He was too busy being nice to Mister P. to even notice me. I went to watch the game, too, didn't I? I shouted and cheered. I mean, I wasn't as cool as the polar bear, I get that, but I tried."

"I think Austin was just trying to be friendly," said Mom. "You know, like when you meet people in the park and they tell you what a lovely dog you've got. It's kind of a good way to get chatting."

Joe sighed. Maybe Mom was right. Maybe not.

"School starts on Monday," said Dad. "Don't forget people need time to get to know *you*. Don't be too quick to judge or take offence or they'll be quick to judge you in return."

"I'm not on trial," said Joe. "The only problem is that there's lots of them and only one of me."

"There's only one of everyone," said Mom. "And if you give everyone a chance, they'll give you a chance too. Just be your normal cheerful self and join in and you'll be fine. Just like Mister P."

"Oh, don't you start as well. Mister perfect P. Perhaps you should just send him to school and dump me in the woods."

Mom raised her eyebrows. Joe folded his arms across his chest and squeezed. He wanted to be his usual cheerful self but he was finding it difficult here. And his parents weren't helping. Everything was so simple before and he'd never had to try that hard. Now it seemed like even his parents had started to doubt him. It looked like he really was going to have to do this alone. He looked in the rearview mirror and saw the huge happy shape of Mister P. reflected back at him.

Joe took a deep breath. "I'll be fine," he said with a dismissive shrug. "I don't know what you're all getting so wound up about."

CHAPTER 9

FEARS AND TEARS

The principal, Mrs. Mills, had suggested an orientation morning so that Joe would have a chance to get used to his new school before he was *thrown in at the deep end* (her words, not his, and he thought she might have come up with something more encouraging).

Arriving at a new school was, Joe decided, like being an alien arriving on another planet. Everything was new and unfamiliar—obviously. Some people stared at you as if you were . . . well, an alien! Others ignored you completely, as if you were invisible. Some were sooperdooper nice to you, but only in an "*I-have-to-be-nice-to-you-because-you're-the-new-kid*" kind of way, while others said absolutely nothing or, worse still, suddenly stopped talking when you were in hearing distance. Maybe it was just Joe's imagination, but things didn't seem that friendly. But then again, maybe he was being unrealistic. He'd never done "new school" before, or not that he could remember, and he didn't really know what to expect. He looked around for Austin, keen to see a familiar face, but there was no sign of him.

Joe was given a tour of the school by a boy called Mitchell and a girl called Tay. Tay was quiet and seemed very efficient. Mitchell was bouncy and full of energy and, Joe decided, definitely knew he was cool. He envied the easy way Mitchell chatted to people as he passed, high-fiving them and saying, "Catch you later." It was like everybody wanted a bit of Mitchell.

The school was about five times the size of his
school back at home and there was a lot to take in.
Tay asked him questions about where he'd come from
and why he'd moved here and where he was living.
Mitchell asked him about games, music, and movies.
Joe never had time for more than a quick answer
because they kept moving from room to room with
Mitchell or Tay giving a quick run-down of what
happened in each one. There was even a music block,
which Joe definitely hadn't had in his last school.

"Do you play an instrument?" asked Mitchell.

"Guitar," said Joe.

"Me too," said Mitchell.

Joe wanted to know more, but they were heading off in another direction and the conversation had already moved on.

"Now for the really exciting bit," said Mitchell, flinging open some double doors and spreading his hands in a dramatic way. "*This* is the school canteen. We all eat in here, whether you have school lunches or not. Apparently eating outside risks attracting the bears."

Joe laughed.

"Not joking, dude," said Mitchell, shaking his head and making claws with his hands. "And I'll tell you something for free—you do NOT want to come face to face with a bear in the school yard."

"Mitchell, stop it," said Tay, looking slightly nervous.

Joe thought this might be a good time to bring up the subject of Mister P., but something about Mitchell made him hesitate. He worried he might make a fool of himself.

"Take my advice," said Mitchell, turning down his mouth and wrinkling his nose. "Don't have school lunches unless you absolutely have to. They're really bad!" He spun around and burst back out through the canteen door, almost leaving it to swing back in Joe's face, but catching it just in time and apologizing.

"They have just started doing *healthy* salads," Tay added.

"Healthy as in more slug than salad," said Mitchell, "and I'd like to know what's healthy about eating slugs."

Joe laughed and remembered one of his jokes. "What's worse than finding a caterpillar in your lettuce?"

"Finding half a caterpillar?" Mitchell fired back and rolled his eyes. "Haven't heard that one since first grade."

Joe wished he'd kept his mouth shut. Now he *had* made a fool of himself. He tried to convince himself that he didn't care what Mitchell thought—that Mitchell was just one of those boys who knew he was cool and liked to make sure everyone else knew they were uncool. But Mitchell seemed too nice for that, which annoyed Joe even more.

As they rounded another corner, Mitchell spotted a group of students heading down towards the music block. He waved at them. "I won't be long," he hollered. "Start without me, if you want." He turned to

Joe. "Do you mind if Tay shows you round the last bit by herself. I've got band practice now and I'd rather not be late. There's not much of the school left to see." Mitchell didn't wait for Joe to answer. "I'll catch you later," he said, raising a hand and sprinting off after the others.

That was *it! Band practice?* The big bomb of frustration that had been building inside Joe ever since they first stepped off the aeroplane suddenly exploded. Watching Mitchell having so much fun, being so popular, rushing off to band practice was not what Joe needed right now. It reminded Joe of everything he'd left behind and made him sick with jealousy. At this moment, he just wanted to BE Mitchell. He could already picture himself playing with the band and going round school high-fiving and laughing and smiling and not telling pathetic first grade jokes.

But, instead, he was trailing obediently after Tay as she chattered on about the maths challenge and how her team had won last year. Joe was fine at maths, but he certainly wouldn't be picked for a maths challenge team. In fact, he probably wouldn't be picked for anything.

By the time they reached the principal's office, Joe had decided he didn't want to be at this school at all.

"I'm sure you're going to like it here," said Tay.

I'm sure I'm not, thought Joe to himself, as he smiled and nodded and thanked Tay for showing him round.

Tay knocked on the principal's door. "All done, Mrs. Mills," she said in a sweeter than sweet voice when the door opened. She stood aside to let Joe go in. His parents were already there.

"Ah, Joe," said Mrs. Mills in a friendly way. "Perfect timing. Come in and join us. I've just been having a chat with your parents. I hope you enjoyed your tour?"

Joe had not enjoyed his tour. "It was great, thank you."

"So, do you have any questions?" she asked.

Joe's parents looked at him expectantly. He did have questions, but none of them were for Mrs. Mills. He shook his head.

"Well, if we're all happy then it looks like you can join us tomorrow."

The trouble was Joe wasn't happy. He wondered how he'd ever feel a part of this school; how he'd ever fit in and make friends. He knew his parents would tell him that it would all take time, but Joe wasn't in the mood to be patient. He tapped the ends of his fingers together and thought about a plan. A plan that would definitely make him Mr. Popular.

"There is one thing," he said, looking more at Mom and Dad than Mrs. Mills. "I think it would be good to have some help—you know, in settling in." He saw Mom's and Dad's eyes widen in concern.

"Is there something you're not telling us?" asked Mom.

"No. It's just I was wondering, perhaps, if bringing a friend to school would make things easier. It would be a good way to help me feel like I belonged."

"A friend?" said Mrs. Mills and Mom at the same time.

Dad frowned at Joe and then laughed, nervously. Joe raised his eyebrows. He was pretty certain Dad knew the friend he had in mind.

"Ah!" Mrs. Mills wagged her finger at Joe. "Your dad has warned me about your sense of humour." She gave Joe a bright smile. "Of course, we'd be delighted if you wanted to bring a "friend" along." As she said the word friend, she drew little speech marks with her fingers. "I'll add him—or her—to the school register, shall I?"

"Him," said Joe. "And I'm not joking."

Dad narrowed his eyes.

"First name," said Mrs. Mills, still laughing, pen at the ready.

"Mister," said Joe. He could see Dad take a deep breath.

"Mister?" said Mrs. Mills. "That's unusual. And his surname?"

"P."

"As in . . . ?" she wrinkled her nose. It was clear that Mrs. Mills thought this was all rather funny.

"As in the letter P," said Joe, not smiling at all.

"And Mister P. would be . . ."

"A polar bear," said Joe. "You'll love him. Everybody does."

Dad's eyebrows shot through the roof and Mrs. Mills threw her head back and laughed, flamboyantly, adding a note to the register. It was only when Mom politely explained that Joe was being serious that Mrs. Mills' smile faded.

"I'm not sure I understand . . ." she said, slowly putting down her notebook.

"I can't even believe we are having this conversation," said Dad.

"Well," said Mom, "I suppose having Mister P. at school with Joe could be a good idea. If Joe says he needs help settling in then we should listen to him." Mom looked at Dad and then at Mrs. Mills.

Mrs. Mills sat up tall. "You need to understand, Mrs. Beechcroft, that our school has a very strict policy on bears."

"Yes, but surely that doesn't include *polar*

bears," said Joe. "Mister P. is completely different. He's just the kind of bear you want around school. He might even keep the other bears away. We could introduce him to you if you like—he's waiting at the school gates right now." Joe nodded towards the window.

Mrs. Mills peered out and fanned herself with her notebook. "This is most unusual," she said. "I really don't know what to say."

"Unusual, but important," said Mom. "It'll only be for a few days. Just until he's settled in."

Mrs. Mills flopped back into her chair and gave a long drawn-out sigh. "I suppose we *could* give it a try. On the strict understanding that you will be responsible for him at all times and that he doesn't set foot in the school canteen. That is a complete no-go area for animals. Do I make myself clear?"

"Clear as a clear blue sky," said Joe.

Mrs. Mills seemed more comfortable now she was back in control. She rearranged her face to look happy and turned to Mom and Dad.

"Well, we look forward to seeing Joe and Mister P. tomorrow. Before 8.30 please. We do not tolerate lateness—although we may make some exceptions." Her eyes drifted to Joe's chair and then back to Mom and Dad.

"I won't be late," said Joe pointedly. "It is my own responsibility to get myself to school on time—so you can speak to me and not my parents."

Dad's mouth dropped open and Mrs. Mills

blinked hard. "Good," she said with a slight edge to her voice. "Well I hope you, and Mister P., will make a positive contribution to our school."

* * *

"Good grief, Joe," said Dad as soon as they were back outside the school gates. "What on earth has got into you? You can't speak to your new principal like that. First all the Mister P. stuff and then . . . I can't believe how rude you were."

"Mrs. Mills needs to learn that if she's got something to say to me, she can say it to my face. You've always told me I have to make people understand that. And she agreed to Mister P. coming to school, so I can't see the problem."

"Are you trying to make your life difficult?"

Joe closed his eyes and all he could see was Mitchell sprinting off to band practice with his friends. "Moving here made my life difficult," said Joe. "Mister P. is the only thing that makes it easier."

A freezing wind threaded its way through the metal fence surrounding the school, making a steely, whining sound.

Mom looked close to tears.

Dad softened a little. "This move isn't easy for any of us, Joe. Your mom and I have got to settle into a new life too. You're not the only one who has left friends and family behind. This is a new world for us as well. You need to realize that this is not all about you. You could learn something from that polar bear. You haven't seen him being grumpy and rude and spoilt, have you?"

Joe looked at the bear, then back at Mom and Dad. Had Joe been acting grumpy and rude and spoilt? He decided maybe he had. Mom started sobbing quietly, wiping her eyes on the back of her sleeve. Mister P. stretched out his paw and reached carefully into Dad's pocket, spearing Dad's handkerchief on the end of his claw. He held it out to Mom who took it and blew her nose. Joe wasn't used to seeing Mom so upset or Dad so angry. He realized he hadn't stopped for one second to think about how his parents might be feeling. He'd been too busy blaming them for everything and feeling sorry for himself. He was so used to his parents always being on his side and now it felt like a big wall had come between the three of them.

Mister P. stepped forward and put a hairy arm around Mom and Dad and another around Joe and swept them all in to a tight circle, curling himself around them in a huge, polar bear hug.

"I'm sorry," said Dad after a few moments.

"I'm sorry too," said Joe.

"Me too," snivelled Mom.

Joe wasn't quite sure what they were all sorry for. Maybe they had all been bottling everything up inside and suddenly it had all started to spill over. Maybe they'd all been too busy trying to survive to think about anyone else. But one thing was quite clear, it was going to take time to settle in this new place and, until they had, they needed to stick together.

That evening Joe sat side-by-side on the deck with Mister P. Being close to the bear made him comfortable. He was glad he'd be taking Mister P. to school with him. Without him, he'd be dreading tomorrow even more. Mister P. looked out across the mountains and rested a paw on Joe's shoulder.

Joe had to admit, the view was breathtaking.

"Maybe I'll learn to love those mountains one day," he said.

The red sun dipped down behind the dark peaks, making the sky and Mister P.'s fur turn pink. It would be the last time they'd see the sun for a few weeks.

CHAPTER 10

UKES AND NUKES

Joe started full-time school the next day. It was a Tuesday filled with cold, gray, and drizzle which made Joe even more grateful for the company of a warm, friendly bear. He was right about Mister P.—everyone wanted to get to know him. For his part, Mister P. behaved in a Mister Perfect way. You'd have thought he'd been at school all his life. He joined in when he was supposed to join in and kept quiet when he was supposed to keep quiet. Wherever Joe went in the school, people wanted to stop and say hello.

Joe had hoped Mister P. might make an impression on Mitchell and give Joe a chance to get to know him better. But Mitchell always seemed to be rushing here or there and was forever telling Joe he'd *catch him later*. The trouble was, he never did.

Lunchtimes were the worst. Each day, when the lunch bell rang, Joe would take Mister P. out to the playground then head slowly to the canteen. By the time he arrived, the room was always crowded and noisy. At his old school, he'd always had tons of friends to sit with, but now he had no one. He hated the long seconds as he stared around trying to decide whether to try and join a table that was already half-full and risk being turned away, or face the humility of sitting at a table by himself. He hoped someone might spot him and wave him over, but without Mister P. by his side, no one seemed to notice him at all.

By the end of the week, Joe would have happily skipped lunch altogether rather than face the agony of the canteen. On Friday, like every day, he took Mister P. out to the playground then tried to summon up the courage to eat lunch alone yet again.

Mister P. nuzzled him with his nose, pushing him gently towards the door.

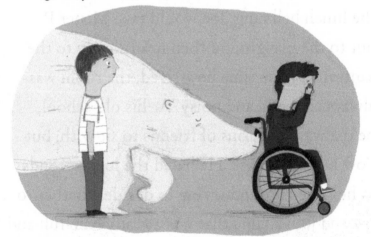

"I can't," said Joe. "I really, really can't. You don't know what it's like in there. I know polar bears are solitary creatures, but humans aren't. Especially me." He felt a tear slip down his cheek and then another.

"Is everything OK?" said a voice behind him. Joe wiped his eyes and turned his head. It was Austin. He'd hardly seen Austin since he'd started and he was embarrassed Austin had caught him crying.

"Yeah, we're fine thanks," said Joe.

Austin hesitated. "You'd better not hang around for too long or you'll get into trouble for being late to lunch."

Joe shrugged. "I think I'm going to stay out here with Mister P."

Austin turned to go, but stopped again. "Come on," he said. "We can go together. Unless you want to carry on avoiding me, that is."

"I'm not—" Joe stopped. Is that what Austin thought? That Joe had been avoiding him? He supposed he hadn't made much of an effort— not with Austin, not with anyone. He'd just let Mister P. do it all for him.

"I'm sorry," said Joe. "I haven't seen you around, that's all."

Austin smiled. "Too busy trying to make friends with Mitchell?"

Joe shook his head. "No . . . no . . ." His cheeks flushed red.

"Whatever," said Austin, smiling. "Are you coming or not?"

Mister P. gave Joe a gentle shove in Austin's direction and Joe followed him down the long corridor to the canteen. They didn't speak on the way and Joe wondered if Austin would abandon him once they arrived.

"Do you want to join us?" said Austin, pointing at a table halfway down the room.

Joe breathed a sigh of relief. "Thanks."

There were three others at the table, Lettie, Buzz, and . . . Conrad. Joe was glad he could remember

their names. "Hi," they all said, breaking off their conversation as they shifted to make room for Joe.

"We're just discussing the Battle of the Bands competition," said Lettie. "It happens at the end of this term. We've got to try and get our act together so we don't come last again, like last year."

"We had a music competition at my old school," Joe volunteered with a burst of enthusiasm. "My band won last year. It was **brilliant.**"

There was a silence around the table. Joe looked down. Perhaps he'd said something wrong. "I mean, you know, it was just a school thing. Nothing amazing." He tried not to sound too pleased with himself.

Lettie smiled. "Congratulations. Maybe you can give us a few pointers then. Tell us your winning secrets!"

Joe wasn't sure whether or not she was being sarcastic.

"Perhaps Joe should join our ukulele band," said Austin. "We could do with *someone* good at music, and when I was at your place the other day, your mom said you were good at music, didn't she?"

It was all Joe could do not to spit out his mouthful of food. Him? Joe? Playing the ukulele? It was nice of Austin to ask and all that, but REALLY? He chewed slowly and swallowed, giving himself time to think.

"So are you good at music?" asked Lettie, an excited look on her face.

Joe wasn't sure how to answer. "Yeah, I'm pretty good. I don't play the ukulele though," he added.

"That doesn't matter," said Buzz. "We can't really play the ukulele either!"

They all laughed.

"So what do you play," said Conrad.

"I play lead guitar," Joe said. "You know, like in a proper band."

Lettie puffed out her cheeks. "Oh, *lead* guitar," she said making the word "lead" last for a long time. "In a *proper* band. I suppose that makes you too good for us. You'd probably be better off talking to Mitchell."

Austin waved his sandwich at Lettie. "He's spent most of this week trying to talk to

Mitchell. But why would anyone want to join Mitchell's band if they could join ours?"

That made everyone laugh some more.

"What's wrong with Mitchell's band?" asked Joe.

"Nothing," said Buzz and Conrad at exactly the same time. "That is the problem. Mitchell's band is out-of-this-world brilliant and they win everything."

"And we come last," said Austin with a grin.

Joe looked over at Mitchell and felt a familiar surge of jealousy. He wanted to tell Austin

and the others that his band at home had been out-of-this-world brilliant and that they had won everything too. But he decided that would sound like he was bragging.

"Apparently," said Austin, still waving his sandwich around at Joe, "If you can play guitar, it's easy enough to pick up the ukulele. So you wouldn't have a problem if you fancied joining us."

"I'm not sure I'm a ukulele kind of person," said Joe, trying not to sound mean.

Lettie folded her arms and leant back in her chair. "Well you're not going to get to play with Mitchell, if that's what you're thinking, because they've been practising all summer. So unless you're going to start up by yourself, you may as well give us a chance. You never know, you might have fun."

Joe picked up a carrot stick from his lunch box and bit off a chunk. It wasn't that he didn't like Austin's group, he just didn't think he wanted to be labelled a loser right from the start.

"What's your band called?" he asked.

"THE NUKES," they all said together.

"The Nukes?" said Joe. "Well that's got an explosive ring to it! Something to make the competition go with a

bang!"

Joe laughed and everyone laughed with him and that made Joe feel good. He could almost feel his old self coming back again.

"Come on," said Austin, leaning forward towards Joe. "We may be more about having fun than winning or losing, but who knows, we could actually get better."

"We're going to sign up Mister P., too," said Lettie. "We think he'll bring in lots of extra votes."

Joe tried to imagine Mister P. performing on stage with a ukulele band. His claws would break all the strings in a nanosecond. Still, maybe that would win votes!

"How often do you practise?" said Joe.

They all looked at each other. "Every now and again,' said Lettie.

"Once in a blue moon," said Buzz.

"At least once every few weeks," said Conrad.

Joe shook his head, thinking of the endless evenings of practice he'd done with the band at home.

"We could do more," said Austin. "Anyway, we haven't got to register until the beginning of next week. If you want to join us, you're in. I think you could make all the difference. Mitchell needs some competition."

Joe sensed four pairs of eyes watching him. He wondered if they'd talked about this before asking him. He glanced over towards Mitchell's table and Mitchell happened to catch his eye and smiled. Joe needed some time to think this over. He picked up his apple, rubbed it on his sleeve, then put it in his pocket.

"For Mister P.," he said when he saw Lettie watching him.

"Oh, he can have mine too," said Buzz, picking up his own apple.

"And mine," said Conrad.

"And mine," said Austin.

Joe watched as everyone put their apple in their pocket. It looked like it was going to be the bear's lucky day. They left the canteen together and went outside to the playground. Austin disappeared, briefly, but joined them a few minutes later, holding a black case in his hand. He held it out to Joe.

"Here. You can borrow this to try it out over the weekend. It's my ukulele."

Joe hesitated, but Mister P. stepped forward, stretched out his long neck, and took the black case between his teeth. He put it on the ground right beside Joe and blinked twice. Then he sat down and nudged Joe's pocket. Joe handed over his apple and Lettie, Buzz, Conrad, and Austin all followed suit. Mister P.'s eyes twinkled as he stared down at the five apples in his paws. He tossed one into the air and then another, juggling all five until he went completely cross-eyed and let them fall into his open mouth. Everybody laughed and clapped and Mister P. gave a proud burp.

That was what life felt like sometimes, Joe decided. A juggling act. The first week of school was almost over and it was ending a little better than he'd expected. He looked at Austin's ukulele on the ground beside him. He liked Austin and the rest of the Nukes, they were good fun, but he still wasn't sure he wanted to play the ukulele in their band. Not sure at all.

Dear Ellie and Noah.

Well it's Friday evening and I've just finished my first week at school. It didn't start too well, I'm not going to lie, but maybe things are starting to get better.

I do have one BIG problem. Austin Wildman (the one who gave me the ice hockey tickets) has asked me to join his ukulele group for the school's Battle of the Bands. The thing is, even though they seem nice, I think I'd rather die than play in a ukulele band. Worse still, the band is really bad and they always come last.

There's another band—a proper band sort of like ours, I'm guessing, but it's run by this boy called Mitchell and he's not likely to be inviting me to join any time soon.

HELP ME! I'm DOOMED!

Joe

Joe hoped one of them would still be awake. It was about ten minutes before a message pinged back.

To: Joe

From: Ellie

HELLO! You've only been at school a week and you've been invited to join a band? That's brilliant. It wouldn't matter if they only played biscuit tins. Anyway, the ukulele is easy to learn, especially if you can play guitar . . . which you can! There are lessons online, I've checked (you know me!) and attach link below.

Love Ellie

p.s. My mom says we can't always expect the world to change just to suit us so sometimes we have to change to suit the world. I'm not exactly sure what she means, but it sounds like good advice.

p.p.s. Mitchell doesn't know what he's missing!

Joe could hear Ellie's voice as he read her email. She was right. Mitchell didn't even know he played guitar. He sighed.

Another message arrived in his inbox.

To: Joe

From: Noah

Chill out! And don't be rude about the ukulele because my mom plays in a ukulele band and they are really cool.

Noah

p.s. Your band will probably be more fun than ours is now that Suzy's joined. She wants to do everything her way. But it's our band and she's

the new band member so she should do it our way, right?

Joe read both messages again. He was sort of glad Suzy was being a pain. It made him feel like he was being missed. And he didn't know Noah's mom played the ukulele. He looked at the black case on the floor and decided maybe he *should* give it a go.

Joe logged on to Ellie's **teach-yourself-ukulele** site and studied the computer screen. He slowly plucked at the strings of the instrument. It made a very different sound to the guitar and it felt quite different to play. "OK, here goes, Mister P. This is going to be my first ever tune on the ukulele. Prepare to be impressed!"

Joe **strummed** and **hummed** his way very badly through a tune, stopping and starting, while Mister P. tapped his paw up and down on the floor.

"Well?" said Joe as he struggled to the end. "What d'you reckon? Not too bad for a first go?" Mister P. scrunched up his paw into a fist and Joe smiled, scrunching up his own hand and giving Mister P. a friendly fist bump.

"Thanks for the encouragement. I'm going to need it if I join Austin's band."

Joe kept strumming away, experimenting with random chords. "I wish I could start my first week at school again," said Joe, thinking out loud as he played, "I think I'd do better second time round." He stopped playing and looked at Mister P. "It was never going to work hiding behind you all the time, was it?"

Mister P. lifted his head and tipped it to one side.

"I'm glad you were there though. Thank you."

Mister P. closed his eyes as Joe stroked the top of his head. Joe decided the bear looked happy. "You've settled in OK, haven't you?" said Joe with a smile. "But maybe this place isn't so strange for you."

Mister P. opened one eye and Joe dangled the ukulele in front of him. "So what do you think? Should I join the Nukes? I mean, it's not exactly the image I'm going for, is it?"

Mister P. stuck his black tongue between his teeth and blew a large raspberry, splattering Joe with polar bear dribble.

"What was that for?" asked Joe, wiping the back of his hand across his face. "Does that mean you think I shouldn't join the Nukes?"

Mister P. blew another raspberry.

"OK, OK, I get it. You think I *should* join. Now stop spitting at me, will you?"

CHAPTER 11
LAKES AND FLAKES

Since the beginning of the week, the weather had turned colder and colder and the gray-blue lake behind the house had transformed into a hard, icy white. When Joe opened the window the air was frosty enough to freeze your nose off. Luckily inside was as warm as toast.

Mister P. couldn't keep still. He kept wandering out into the backyard, looking up at the sky, then wandering back again. In and out. In and out. Joe kept an eye on him, following his movements and wondering what he was searching for. It was a thick black night, with no moon or stars in sight. Joe was feeling pretty restless himself. He had the whole weekend ahead of him without a plan. As he let Mister P. back in for the fifth time, he heard the phone ring and a while later Dad came into his room, looking happy. "That was Simon Wildman calling. He and Austin have invited us on a fishing expedition tomorrow."

"A *fishing* expedition?" spluttered Joe. "What kind of fishing expedition?"

Joe didn't know if it was the word fishing or the sound of Dad's excitement, but Mister P. was suddenly paying a lot of attention.

"We're going to head north. According to Simon, it's pretty wild up there and there's an amazing lake, he says, with huge fish." Dad spread his hands to show the size of the fish. Mister P. copied Dad, spreading his paws even wider. "It'll be good to have a change of scene. It's kind of the Wildmans to invite us and it may be our last chance. Apparently you can't get up there once winter has really set in."

"Winter *has* really set in," said Joe. "It's freezing out there. And how am I supposed to get around in this wild place? Why can't the Wildmans invite us to do something sensible like go to the movies or ten-pin bowling?"

"It'll be fine, I'm sure," said Dad. "We can try out the new freewheel for your chair. That should make it easier to navigate the rough ground and any snow."

"Rough ground *and* snow?" Joe looked at Dad. Dad was normally super-cautious, super-worried, super-protective. "Dad, are you feeling all right?"

"It shouldn't be too snowy," said Dad, with a shrug. "And apparently once we're on the lake, it will be smooth and flat."

"ON the lake?" said Joe, his eyes wide. Apparently, Dad really *was* losing it.

"The lake is frozen solid. Like an ice rink," replied Dad.

"So how do we fish then?"

"I guess we'll find out. All part of the adventure. Mom's gone to pick up some essentials from town and the Wildmans are bringing all the fishing gear. We leave first thing tomorrow morning."

"Great," said Joe, trying hard to sound enthusiastic. Once Dad had left the room, he hid his face in his hands. Dad had never forced him to go on adventures at home—going to the park was about as adventurous as it got. "Fishing on a frozen lake in the middle of nowhere, Mister P.? It sounds nuts to me."

Mister P. nudged his nose gently against Joe's hands until Joe lifted his head.

"I get why you're excited about this, Mister P.," he said. "But you have to realize you are a polar bear and I am very definitely not. I've never even tried my chair in snow. What if I can't move?"

Mister P. gave a huge sigh, stood up, and trotted over to the window, pushing it wide open and letting a blast of cold air into the room.

"Now what are you doing? It's freezing out there."

Mister P. pushed his head out as far as he could.

Joe joined Mister P. at the window and tried to look out, but it wasn't easy with a polar bear in the way. "I know you like the cold, but would you mind if we closed the window before my room turns into a deep freeze?"

Mister P. reversed slowly and pulled his head back in so he was nose to nose with Joe. Resting on the very tip of Mister P.'s nose was a single, beautiful snowflake. Mister P. looked at it and grinned, going slightly cross-eyed.

Joe watched as the snowflake melted into a tiny drop of water and slid to the floor.

"So is this where winter really sets in?" he said, touching the end of Mister P.'s black nose.

He looked out into the darkness where a few random snowflakes were drifting towards the ground. "Time for Joe to get to grips with the snow." Joe tried to mimic Austin's accent as he spoke. "Looks like our adventure may have just got more adventurous."

Mister P. hopped from foot to foot and Joe laughed and pulled the window closed. "Ice and snow is your territory, Mister P. I hope you're ready with some handy tips because I'm going to need all the help I can get!"

Mister P. slid slowly to the ground, looked up at Joe, and grinned.

CHAPTER 12
LIFTS AND DRIFTS

Something was different. He could tell the minute he opened his eyes. It wasn't just that Mister P. was rushing round the room like an over-excited furball. It was something to do with the light.

Mister P. clamped Joe's covers between his teeth and ripped it off the bed.

"Hey, give me a break!" Joe tried to grab back his covers. "It's 7:30 in the morning and it's the weekend. I know we're going fishing, but this is ridiculous."

Mister P. scooted over to the window and

clapped his paws together. Joe sat up and rubbed his eyes.

"Wow! WOW!"

Joe's heart beat fast. This was amazing. The world outside had changed overnight and where there'd been green and gray and brown, now everything was covered in a thin coating of crisp, white, sparkling snow.

Mister P. hurtled to the bedroom door and let himself out. A few moments later, Joe heard the back door open and soon Mister P. appeared outside in the backyard. The bear raced round and round and round, kicking up the snow, and making a maze of pawprints across the ground. He gathered a pile of snow together in his paws and then threw it towards Joe's window where it landed with a splat against the glass.

"What is going on in here?" said Dad, appearing at the doorway in his pajamas.

Joe smiled and pointed to the window. Dad stood with his hands on his hips and roared with laughter. "Polar bear playtime," he said and flung open the window . . . precisely at the same time as Mister P. lobbed another snowball through the air. It hit Dad smack on the chest, covering Joe's carpet with a sprinkle of white crystals.

"Oi," laughed Dad. "Two can play at that game." He scooped a handful of snow off the window ledge and threw it back at Mister P.

"Can we go out?" asked Joe.

"Yes, why not?" replied Dad, and he helped Joe out of bed and clipped the extra wheel into place on his chair. He threw a sweater at Joe and shoved some sneakers onto his feet. Joe didn't wait for Dad to put on his own boots. He raced to the door, teetered at the top of the ramp then skidded down at full speed.

"Aaaaahhhhhhhh!"

He slammed to a stop with his face buried deep in Mister P.'s chest.

"Thanks, Mister P.," he mombled, though it came out sounding nothing like that because his mouth was stuffed with polar bear fur.

Mister P. pushed him out into the snow and spun him round and round then galloped off to make more snowballs. Moving about was much easier with a freewheel, but it didn't make it any easier for Joe to dodge the snowballs as they flew in his direction. Dad jogged out looking pretty silly in his pajamas and a pair of boots. He scooped up handfuls of snow and passed them to Joe, who lobbed them one by one at Mister P.

Mister P. ducked and dived until finally one of Joe's snowballs hit him with a big *boof* on the nose. Mister P. staggered around making a huge drama, finally

falling onto his back and flapping his front
and hind legs through the snow, making one
enormous snow angel.

"My turn," shouted Joe. Dad looked at Joe,
shrugged his shoulders, lifted him from his

chair, and put him on the ground next to Mister P. Joe lay down and waved his arms up and down and Dad dived into the snow next to him and did the same. It was FREEZING, but it was FUN. Joe didn't care that he was numb with cold because he was laughing so much.

"What are you all doing?" shrieked Mom from the door. "Are you trying to give yourselves hypothermia? Get back in here this minute."

Joe, Dad, and Mister P. sat up and grinned, but as soon as the cold air hit his back, Joe realized just how cold he was. Dad raced him back into the house.

"Time for a hot shower, I think," whispered Dad. "Then off for the fishing trip."

Joe's excitement dwindled away. He'd rather spend the day mucking about in the snow at home than going off to some frozen lake to try to catch fish he didn't want to catch.

By the time he'd got out of his shower, Mom had laid out an array of clothing on the bed. Joe took one look and backed away.

"Mom! That's the kind of things toddlers wear. No way. Absolutely NO WAY am I putting on a onesie snowsuit and furry boots."

Mom folded her arms and added his bobble hat and a pair of thick gloves. Joe groaned. This was going to be worse than embarrassing. He was not going to meet Austin looking like a complete twit.

Joe cast his eyes around the room, searching for his favourite hoodie.

"Looking for this?" said Mom picking it up off the floor. "Urrrgh! I only washed it a couple of days ago and now it's covered in polar bear fur."

"All the better for keeping warm," said Joe, grabbing it out of Mom's hands.

Mom helped Joe throw on his clothes and left him pulling his hoody over his head. She told him breakfast would be ready in five minutes.

Joe hid the onesie snowsuit and bobble hat under his pillow and carried the snow boots through to the kitchen. He wolfed down porridge and hot chocolate, keeping an eye on Mom and Dad as they rushed around gathering blankets and food and stuff for the car. Mister P. waited by the door, his own bobble hat pulled on to his

head and his paw resting on his suitcase.

He'd obviously seen everyone else packing up and decided to do the same.

"Don't get your hopes up," said Joe, eyeing the case. "It may look as though we're packing to go away on a month's vacation, but we're only driving an hour north. You certainly won't be needing your swimming trunks."

Mister P. drummed his claws on the case and waited while Mom and Dad finished all the preparations. Joe packed up the sandwiches and snacks and made his way cautiously outside, Mister P. walking just one step in front of him in case of any slips and slides. The sky was a beautiful blue and everything sparkled in the sun. Even a fishing trip seemed more appealing on a day like today.

Dad had already heated up the car and Mister P. took up his usual position in the back. Mom stood in the front door, still wearing her dressing gown and looking a little hassled.

"You have got your snowsuit with you, haven't you, Joe?"

Joe held up a snow boot and pretended to check in the back seat of the truck. "Yep," said Joe. "It's all in a safe place." He decided that saying it like that made it less of a lie. Under his pillow seemed like a safe enough place.

"See you later," shouted Dad, raising his hand in farewell.

"Take care," said Mom, wrapping her arms around her front. "Keep warm and please don't do anything stupid."

She waved them off and, from the worried look on her face, you'd have thought she was NEVER going to see them again.

CHAPTER 13

DRILLS, THRILLS, AND SPILLS

Worrying about doing things was usually much worse than actually doing them—that's what Ellie always said—and now they were on the road, Joe agreed. It was cozy in the truck and Mister P. was chilling out, lying on his back with his head propped against the passenger cab and one of his back legs crossed over the other. Obviously this weather suited him.

Dad had put the basket of sandwiches, snacks, and a thermos of hot soup on the seat beside them and Mom had piled the car full of

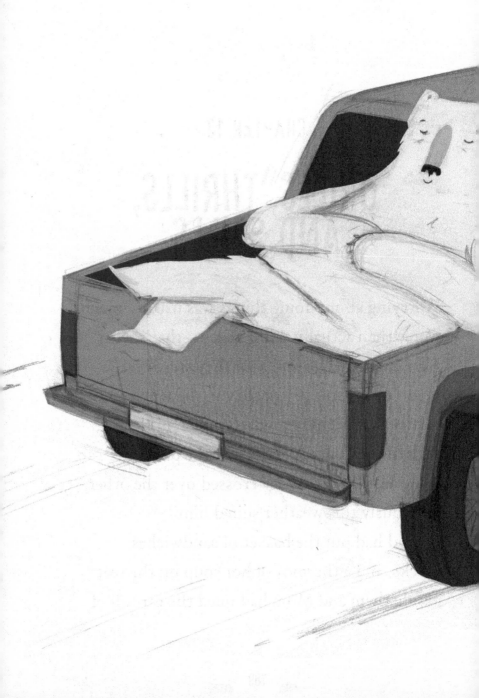

rugs and enough "safety essentials" to support a trip to the North Pole. Joe was beginning to understand why they needed such a large car. They'd arranged to pick up the Wildmans from their house on the other side of town. With a thin covering of snow, the world outside the town looked clean and bright, but once they got to the town itself the white was already turning a slushy brown. They pulled up outside the Wildmans' door and Dad rang the bell.

Austin and his dad appeared, loaded up with fishing kit. Joe stared at them and his stomach sank. He should have listened to Mom. Both Austin and Mr. Wildman were wearing all-in-one snowsuits and thick woolly hats. Austin wasn't looking overly happy and Joe wondered if he was only coming because his dad had told him he had to—both boys being dragged along on this adventure their dads had cooked up.

Austin climbed
into the truck and gave
Joe a high five. They
watched as the dads
loaded even more kit.

"Are we going
for a day or a year?"
whispered Joe.

"Tell me about it,"
said Austin, rolling
his eyes. "Dad says we
have to be prepared for
anything."

"Have you done this before?" asked Joe.

"Ohhhhh yes," said Austin, and Joe tried to read the tone of his voice. "And you?"

"Nope. First time fishing."

"Wow, that's something," said Austin.

The further out of town they drove, the quieter the roads became. Soon they may as well have been the only people on the planet. Main roads turned into narrow tracks with forest on either side—row upon row of pine trees all iced with a thin, sugary layer of snow.

Mister P. sat bolt upright in the back and examined his surroundings with interest. Mr. Wildman talked about the ice hockey and then about fishing. "With ice hockey it's all about noise and activity, with fishing it's all about stillness and silence." Joe decided Mr. Wildman's life revolved around ice. And while Joe had to admit he'd enjoyed the noise and energy of ice hockey, he wasn't sure stillness and silence and freezing temperatures sounded a lot of fun. He looked at Dad, who turned on the radio in the background until the news came on and then the weather forecast.

"We'd better listen in to this," said Mr. Wildman, leaning forward. "It's always good to have a handle on the weather."

At that exact moment, the signal started to crackle and everything became harder to follow. Something about crrrrkkkkk storm unexpectedly changing direction crrrrrrkkkk to be prepared for the worst crrrrkkkkk.

Dad tried, and failed, to get a better signal, then hit the off button. Now the only sound was the heavy wheels slushing along the road.

"Did they say something about a storm coming in?" said Joe, trying to sound laid-back.

"Yeah, but way north of here," said Mr. Wildman. "It'll be like a beach in summer where we're going."

"Good thing Mister P. has brought his

swimming shorts then," said Joe.

"He hasn't, has he?" asked Austin.

Dad rolled his eyes and Joe turned to Austin. "Wait 'til you see what he's got in his suitcase. Sun screen, dark glasses, the lot." He held Austin's eye for a few moments until Austin smiled and shook his head. "You're joking, right?"

"Right," said Joe.

Mr. Wildman kept issuing directions and the track got rougher and rougher. The truck lurched from side to side as it crossed the lumpy, bumpy ground and poor Mister P. struggled to keep his balance as the truck tipped first one way and then the other. Ahead, the trees cleared and a large, solid lake came into view. Dad brought the truck to a stop, pulled on the handbrake, and switched off the engine. Joe opened his door. There was hardly a sound up here in this remote and wild place, and it was definitely nothing like a beach in

summer. It was the kind of place you felt alone and slightly scared, even if there were other people around.

Mr. Wildman and Austin were busy wrapping themselves up in scarves and gloves as fast as they could. As Joe lowered himself out of the truck, an icy wind sliced through his clothes. Dad pulled on his all-in-one suit and then looked at Joe. "Where's yours?" he asked.

Joe didn't know what to say. The cold was bone-cracking. His hoody, jeans, and coat were no match for this. Mister P. jumped out and gave himself a shake. He picked up his suitcase, opened it, and started chucking stuff at Joe with his teeth. Joe's eyes widened.

"You legend, Mister P.," he whispered as he caught first the snowsuit then thick socks, gloves, scarf, and bobble hat.

Austin waited, looking slightly awkward, while Dad helped Joe into all his clothing then handed him an extra jacket. "I brought this along because it's hard to explain to anyone how cold it gets up here. I've grown out of it, but I thought it might fit you."

"Are you calling me *short* by any chance? I am sitting down, you know!"

Austin looked at him, horrified, and started to apologize.

Joe put up his hands and grinned. "Austin! Don't look so worried! I'm just making a *joke*."

Austin stopped and then smiled. "Sorry," he said. "Sometimes you sound so serious, it's hard to know."

Dad nodded at Austin. "You'll soon get used to his sense of humor. He'll give you plenty of practice."

"In the meantime," said Joe, "just to avoid any misunderstanding, I'll give you a small sign like this"—Joe drew a little smile in the air with his finger—"so you know when I'm joking."

Austin nodded and looked embarrassed.

"Thanks for the jacket, by the way," said Joe. "I think I'm going to need it."

Dad threw Joe a blanket to tuck around his legs and Mr. Wildman pointed to an area along the edge of the lake where there was a gentle slope onto the ice. The extra wheel on the front of Joe's chair made it easier—but not easy— to navigate the rough ground. Everyone had to help. They stopped by the edge of the lake and Joe saw Dad hesitate. He'd always told Joe NEVER to go onto ice. What if it cracked? What if he fell through?

Mister P. had no such hesitation, not even for a second. He bounded straight onto the lake, leapt into the air, did a splendid pirouette then skidded to a neat stop and thumped the ice with a large paw. It made a strangely dead sound.

"It's safe," said Austin. "Wait till you see how thick it is."

Mr. Wildman dragged his equipment to a spot near the centre of the lake and began drilling a hole in the ice with what looked like a huge corkscrew. Austin was right, the ice was thicker than he could ever have imagined. Round and round and round went the corkscrew—Mr. Wildman turning redder and redder in the face as he drilled and drilled. Suddenly the plug of ice gave way and fresh water gurgled to the surface. Mister P. poked his nose into the hole and stood very still while Mr. Wildman hoisted the drill onto his shoulder.

"We call this an awl," he said. "A-W-L."

Joe nodded and wondered if he was going to be tested on fishing terminology later on.

"OK, Austin. You show young Joe here how to set up. Let's see if we can't catch ourselves a whopper. Mister P.—having your big snout stuffed in the water there is not going to help."

Mister P. looked up indignantly. Austin gave Joe a nudge. "Mister P. has way more chance of catching a fish than we do," he whispered. He handed Joe the fishing rod and told him to hold it while he put bait on the end of the line. Mister P. kept a careful eye on the boys as they dropped the line through the hole.

"What happens now?" asked Joe.

Austin crossed his arms and sighed. "We all sit and stare at the hole for about five hours is what happens."

"Sounds exciting," said Joe and grinned. "Perfect way to spend a weekend! Staring at a hole."

"Yeah," said Austin. Then he laughed.

Mr. Wildman frowned at them and raised his finger to his lips. **"Shhhhh."**

That made them both laugh even more until Mister P. put a hairy paw over both of their mouths.

Mister P., Austin, and Joe gazed silently down into the dark water. They sat and sat and sat.

They waited . . .
   and waited . . .
     and waited.

NOTHING HAPPENED.

"Having fun?" whispered Austin, banging his gloved hands together trying to warm them up.

"Loving it," mouthed Joe.

Mister P. opened his mouth wide as wide and gave the most enormous yawn. This was SO boring it was actually funny.

Suddenly the line twitched and the shock made Joe pull the rod back fast. Mister P. leapt to his feet. The fishing line was running and running and running away and the reel was spinning and spinning and spinning.

"Woooooooahhhh," shouted Joe, struggling to hold on to the rod.

"Jeeeeepers!!!!" cried Austin, holding on to Joe's chair to give him extra stability.

"HOLD ON!" shouted Mr. Wildman. "You've got a monster there."

"A monster?" gasped Joe.

As the line stopped running, he began to reel in. The weight was incredible. It was too heavy for Joe to do alone and so he and Austin took it in turns. Finally, as Joe and Austin pulled the fish clear of the ice, Mister P. stepped forward. It was the most enormous fish that any of them had ever seen.

"Will you look at that?" said Mr. Wildman. "Good work. You three make a good team."

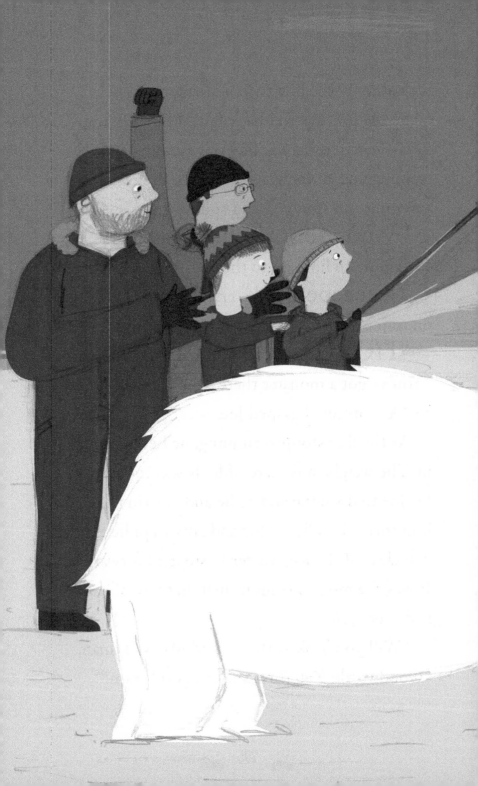

Mr. Wildman and Dad quickly snapped some photos of the boys and Mister P. with their fish. Then Mr. Wildman lay down and gently lowered the animal back through the ice and let him swim away. Joe was pleased to see the fish returned to the water. Mister P. didn't look quite so sure.

"Don't worry," said Joe. "I've got food for you in the truck."

A ripple of wind spread through the pine trees. Mister P. lifted his nose and looked up the lake to the distant sky. The boys followed his gaze. The bear made a strange chuff-chuffing sound and lifted one paw off the ice.

"Something's up," said Joe. They all stopped and looked and listened. The sky above them was a pale gray, but in the distance, rolling towards them, was a dense yellowy-black cloud like nothing Joe had ever seen before. It was almost hypnotizing.

Mister P. tucked his head down between his front legs and growled quietly.

Mr. Wildman frowned and then started to move fast. "It looks like that storm they were talking about may be tracking in our direction. I'd say it's going to hit us good and proper. We need to get out of here—fast. Okay everyone, let's shift it."

Shifting it wasn't as easy as it sounded. The awl was heavy, the rods and lines had to be packed up, the rough ground seemed even harder to navigate. The quicker they tried to do things, the longer it seemed to take. Mr. Wildman was barking orders and Dad was trying to stay cool. Finally, with all the gear, people, and polar bear loaded into the car, Dad started to drive, bouncing and bumping harder and heavier, as they hurtled along the track at twice the speed they had on the way. And all the time the wall of darkness was chasing up the valley behind them.

Joe's heart beat fast. He'd never seen Dad drive like this before and, for some reason, it made him grip his seat and sit very still. The strength of the wind was buffeting the truck and making the branches of the trees dip and sway. Even though it was early afternoon, it felt like evening and Dad peered nervously in his mirror.

"Is Mister P. okay?" asked Joe.

Austin turned and craned his neck so he could see into the back. "He's sitting on the floor of the truck and he's got his head down. I reckon he's staying as low as he can."

"Sensible bear," said Mr. Wildman. "He doesn't want a tree on his head."

"I don't want a tree on my head either," said Joe, fixing his eyes on the swaying branches.

Snowflakes started to fall, light and feathery and friendly at first, then thicker and thicker until the world changed into a breathless, blasting, blinding blizzard.

CHAPTER 14

DRIFTS AND RIFTS

The windshield wipers scraped backwards
and forwards, backwards and forwards, but as
fast as they wiped the snow out of the way, it
kept coming. Even with the headlights on, you
couldn't see more than about four inches ahead.
The wind battered the snow against the glass
and sent it swirling and whirling, leaving Joe
dizzy and disoriented. Dad drove slower and
slower. The road had all but disappeared and it
was impossible to tell where the asphalt ended
and the grass began. Everything was a crazy
world of shadow and white.

Dad peered ahead, trying to get some sense

of direction, but it was useless. "I'm not going to be able to keep going much longer," he said.

Joe looked at him and frowned. "But what are we going to do? We have to get home. We can't stay out in this weather. WE MIGHT DIE.'

"Thanks for pointing that out," said Dad. "Always nice to have an optimistic travel companion!"

Dad was trying to sound funny, but Joe could hear the tension in his voice. Ahead, the road rose in a massive lump of solid white. Dad squinted and muttered something under his breath as he applied the brakes and slid to a halt.

"I guess this is where we stop," said Mr. Wildman. He opened the door, creating a snow storm inside the truck, and clambered out. Not only was it snowing from the sky, but the snow was being lifted from the ground and blown horizontally. Mr. Wildman stumbled towards the mound blocking the road. The

truck creaked and shifted slightly as Mister
P. clambered down and joined him. Mister P.
heaved his huge body against the mound, trying
to shift it out of the way. It was no good. Mr.
Wildman returned to the car. He was covered in
snow and his eyelashes had frozen.

"Tree down," he gasped, slamming the door
behind him and pulling off his woolly hat.
His body steamed in the cold air he'd let into
the truck, fogging up all the windows. "Worst
conditions I've seen in years."

Joe swallowed. "So . . . what does that mean, exactly?" Something about this situation was unreal. As if it was happening to someone else.

"Well," responded Mr. Wildman, leaning forward, "we hope the blizzard will blow through quickly so we can be rescued. But the truth of the matter is we could be here for days."

Joe looked at Austin and drew a little smiley face with his finger and raised his eyebrows. Austin shook his head. OK, so this was NOT a joke. A thousand thoughts raced through Joe's mind—none of them good.

"But why was there no warning?" asked Dad, turning to Mr. Wildman. "The forecast was for a little snow, but not this!"

"These storms can be unpredictable. That's why we travel with emergency provisions. Never had to use them before though."

"Great," said Dad with more than a hint of sarcasm.

"What about Mister P.?" asked Joe.

"Mister P. is the one thing we don't have to worry about," said Dad. "He's got more experience of this kind of thing than the rest of us put together." Mister P. was already busy outside the truck. He seemed to be pushing and piling snow in the space underneath the vehicle.

Mr. Wildman pressed his face up to the window. "The bear knows what he's doing. He's filling the gap under the truck so the cold air can't get in. Believe it or not, the snow will actually keep us warm. We'd better cut the engine, though, and try to conserve fuel. We'll turn it on every now and again to boost the warmth."

Joe glanced at the fuel indicator. It wasn't empty, but it wasn't full either. Dad turned the key and cut the engine. The silence was long and heavy.

"We'll need to check the exhaust pipe at the back is clear," said Austin. "Or we'll all get gassed. They taught us that at school."

Mr. Wildman nodded.

Joe had only felt real fear once before in his life and he knew he never wanted to feel it again. Stuck in a blizzard. Freezing. Risk of being gassed. What else could possibly go wrong?

Dad rubbed his hands up and down his face. "I don't suppose anyone has got any signal on their phone?"

Oh yes, *no phone*. Joe added it to the list. He already knew the answer was NO. It was the first thing he'd checked. His fear turned to anger.

"I told you we shouldn't move to this stupid place. Who'd want to live in a place with weather like this? And I never wanted to come on this stupid fishing trip either."

"Hey, easy!" said Mr. Wildman. "I know you're upset, but there's no need to get personal. Our town is a great place to live and my family has been living happily here for generations."

"And I bet if we came to your hometown, it wouldn't be perfect either. Nowhere is perfect," said Austin.

"At least we have a reliable phone signal where I come from," grumbled Joe. "I mean, that's the whole point, isn't it? When you have an emergency away from home, you're supposed to be able to call someone."

Dad reached across and put his hand on Joe's shoulder. Joe tried to shake it away.

"Joe, now is not the time to start a scene. Think about it. Even if we had a phone signal, no one would get to us in this weather. We can't control everything in life and we certainly can't control the weather. We all agree that this isn't a great situation, but right now we need to stick together and stay calm and we'll all be fine."

Dad sounded a lot calmer than he looked, but Joe knew he was right. Joe's anger disappeared, leaving room for the fear to come back. "Sorry," he mumbled.

"It's normal to feel scared," said Mr. Wildman. "But we have the gear we need, and someone at home will raise the alarm, so all we can do is sit out the storm and wait. It won't be so bad."

Won't be so bad!? Joe thought. *This is like a nightmare!* But out loud he just said, "There must be *something* we can do."

"There's plenty. We're going to wrap ourselves up in these blankets and put on all our spare clothes. We've got plenty of hot soup and food to keep us going and we won't eat it all at once." Mr. Wildman sounded in control and it gave Joe a little more confidence.

Mister P. was still busy behind the truck. It was impossible to see what he was doing. "I hope he's not stuffing snow *into* the exhaust pipe," said Dad. "I'd better check."

Dad slipped out of the truck as fast as he could. Within seconds he was back in again, shaking his head.

"Bad news?" said Mr. Wildman.

"Quite the opposite. That bear is a hero. He's cleared the pipe for us." Dad gave a low whistle of surprise. "Can you believe that? We'll certainly be safe to turn the engine on when we need to."

Joe managed to find a smile. "I bet you're glad I accidentally signed that piece of paper at the airport now."

The wind carried on blowing. And as the snow on the ground got thicker and thicker, the silence got deeper and deeper.

They huddled under the blankets and Mr. Wildman gave everyone a small square of chocolate. For the moment it was warm. "Now all we have to do is keep ourselves cheerful," he said. "Anyone know any good jokes?"

Dad pointed at Joe. "This is your man for jokes," he said.

For a few moments, Joe struggled to think of a single joke. He wondered if his brain had frozen.

"Where do you find a polar bear?" he asked, finally.

"I don't know. Where do you find a polar bear?" said Dad.

"Depends where you lost him," said Joe and started to laugh.

"That's terrible," groaned Dad, but laughed all the same.

"I've got one, I've got one," said Austin. "What did the woolly hat say to the scarf?"

Joe shrugged.

"You hang around and I'll go on a-head!!!!"

Joe laughed, Dad smirked, and Mr. Wildman rolled his eyes.

"What do you call a polar bear wearing ear muffs?" Joe tried. "Call him anything you like, he can't hear you."

Austin burst into the funniest laugh Joe had ever heard. He sounded like a sea lion. And that made everyone else laugh.

"Well, that's broken the ice," said Joe when he managed to take a breath and then dissolved into more giggles. "Broken the ice . . . broken the ice . . . get it?"

Now everyone was helpless with laughter. "That's not even a joke," said Dad. And it wasn't, but it didn't matter, because laughter was good, laughter was catching, and it made Joe feel better. Austin and Joe went backwards and forwards with jokes that got worse and worse. Joe decided Austin might be even funnier than Ellie.

Finally the jokes ran out. The temperature continued to drop and Dad turned on the engine, filling the car with warm air. Then he cut the motor again and the silence returned.

"What's in here?" asked Austin, holding up Mister P.'s battered old suitcase. "It feels heavy."

"I don't know. I thought he just had my spare clothes," said Joe. "Open it up and take a look. I hope he didn't sneak a fish in there."

Joe watched while Austin lifted the lid. Austin frowned and then smiled. "It's my ukulele," he said. "What's he doing with that in his suitcase? D'you think he was planning on putting in a little practice if the fishing got too boring?"

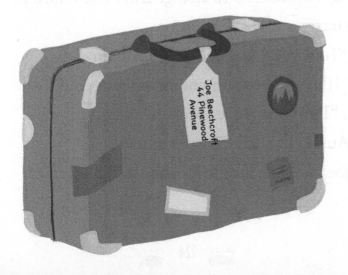

Joe Beechcroft
44 Pinewood Avenue

"Well, you can play us a tune," said Dad. "That will keep us entertained."

Mr. Wildman's face took on a pained expression. "Have you heard him play?" he asked. "It's not quite as entertaining as you might imagine."

Joe didn't think that was very fair. "Go on, Austin. It'll be great."

Austin looked at his Dad and then started to play.

Strum, strum STOP.
Strum, strum STOP.

Joe watched as Austin fumbled with all the fingering for the different chords. It took Austin about ten seconds to change from one chord to the next.

"Told you I was bad," said Austin.

"It's only because your hands are cold," said Joe. "Put your gloves back on and give it here."

Austin handed over the ukulele.

Joe took off his gloves and started to play.

He tried to remember what he'd learned last
night. His warm room and his computer screen
seemed a million miles away now. Still, he
managed to adapt a few songs he knew from the
guitar, and before long Dad had started to sing.

Austin and Mr. Wildman stared at Joe in
amazement.

"You're really good," said Austin. "No kidding."

"So are you," said Joe, trying to sound like he meant it. "And by the time we get to the music competition we'll both be ace."

"Does that mean you're going to join our group?" asked Austin quietly.

"Definitely—if you'll still have me," said Joe. "Perhaps we should change the group's name to **The Blizzards** and give ourselves a new start."

"And all play wearing our snowsuits," added Austin.

"And have Mister P. on stage to add atmosphere," said Joe.

"It's a deal," Austin laughed.

And even though it was cold, Joe felt a little burst of warmth inside.

Joe didn't play for long. The temperature was plummeting again and he needed to keep his hands warm. As the fuel level dropped, Dad turned the car on less and less. Snow continued to pile up outside and as the darkness fell, Joe did his best to think about good things—like winning band competitions— but it was hard and he was scared.

They huddled together and drank hot soup and covered themselves in every blanket they had.

Finally they fell asleep.

CHAPTER 15
LIGHT AND FLIGHT

Joe awoke, cold and stiff, to find the truck almost completely buried in snow. A glimmer of sunlight was just visible, which meant only one thing. The blizzard must have blown through.

Dad tried to open his door but it was stuck. The others tried too, but all the doors were totally blocked by snow. Joe hated being trapped. He needed to get out. He needed to breathe. He bunched up his fists and was about to open his mouth when the truck dipped at the front and two hairy windsheild wipers pushed aside the snow from the front of the car in a couple of hefty sweeps. Mister P.'s large face peered in and he waved with both paws.

The sight of the light and the sun and the bear brought an overwhelming sense of relief and they all gave each other high fives.

"We're stuck!" shouted Joe, pointing at his door.

Mister P. set to work digging huge pawfuls of snow away from the car. Before long he'd cleared Dad's door and then the back doors, and Dad and Mr. Wildman jumped out and began to help shovelling snow. It wasn't long before Joe could lower himself out of the truck.

The scene that met his eyes was hard to take in. The world looked like a moonscape. There wasn't a jagged edge anywhere in sight. It was all sweeping mounds and hummocks and bumps of smooth and sparkling white snow.

Dad looked exhausted, and Mr. Wildman put an arm round his shoulders. "They'll have the search helicopters out. We need to make ourselves visible so they can spot us." Mr. Wildman turned the two side mirrors of the

truck towards the sky to reflect the sun.

"We could use our foil emergency blankets too," said Dad. He removed one from the car and spread it out over the roof of the truck, weighing it down on the four corners with balls of snow.

"And maybe we should try and clear a landing spot," said Mr. Wildman. "That would help a lot and it would warm us up."

Joe swung his arms backwards and forwards, clapping his hands as he watched the others dig. Luckily the snow was light and Mister P. was a machine. He dug at twice the speed of the others. Now they were in the sun, things seemed more hopeful.

"I know," said Austin, "Let's build a snowman making the help sign."

Joe could only watch and make suggestions as Mister P. got stuck in, making a large ball of snow for the body while Austin worked on the head. They broke off a couple of large sticks to make arms in the shape of a V to show that help was needed.

"How does it look?" said Austin

"Perfect," said Joe.

"And just in time," said Dad, holding up his hand. **"Sssshhhhhh."** A distant, steady drumbeat reverberated through the air. Quietly at first, then steadily louder.

Mister P. tipped his nose towards the sky.

"That's the helicopter," said Mr. Wildman. "Wave your arms everybody."

Joe didn't think it was possible to feel so happy. The four of them waved for all they were worth and Mister P. joined in with his large paws. The side mirrors glinted upwards and the foil blanket dazzled.

The helicopter circled once, then twice, and then dropped as low as it could. Mr. Wildman shouted at everyone to take cover while he helped to guide the helicopter in.

The trees shook as the air vibrated with the helicopter blades. Snow crashed from branches and exploded onto the ground. Joe covered his ears and Mister P. stood in front of the little group like a wall of fur, his back to the

helicopter, protecting them from the icy blast.

The blades slowed to a stop and the rescue crew jumped out and ran towards them.

"Two adults, two children, and a polar bear. Is that right?" The man who was in charge checked their names off the list. "Is everyone doing okay?"

"We're all fine," said Mr. Wildman. "Mainly thanks to Mister P. here."

"We need to get you out as soon as we can," the rescuer replied. "We're expecting another wave of snow to come in later this morning."

"What about my truck?" said Dad.

"It'll have to stay here for the time being. The snowplows aren't going to get these roads clear for a few days yet. There's a lot of trees down too."

"Sir," said another of the rescuers. "What do we do with the bear? We're not going to fit him in the helicopter. I think we'll have to put him on the winch."

"The winch?" asked Joe.

"We'll sling him below the helicopter," explained the man. "He'll be quite safe. I'll travel with him."

There wasn't time for Joe to argue. He gave Mister P. a hug.

Mister P. hugged Joe back and wouldn't let go.

"You'll be all right," said Joe. "Be brave, and do as you're told."

Austin, Dad, and Mr. Wildman clambered on board the helicopter and Joe was lifted in and his chair loaded into the back. They all strapped in. Joe could see the rescue man on the ground with Mister P., carefully getting him in to what looked like a giant sling.

The blades started to rotate, picking up speed. The noise was deafening.

"Mister P. isn't going to like this noise," yelled Joe, but his voice was drowned out. He clung to Dad's arm as the helicopter lifted off the ground, then pressed his face to the window, trying to see what was happening to the bear.

As the helicopter rose higher
and higher into the air, Joe got a
bird's eye view of the white world
below. He could just see Mister P.,
suspended beneath the helicopter
at the end of a long wire. The bear
was flying—possibly the first flying
polar bear in history—and he was
grinning his head off.

Austin and Joe gave each other a thumbs up. Joe thought this helicopter ride must be the most exciting thing he'd ever done. As the town came into sight, Joe closed his eyes and sank back into his seat, exhausted. He felt tears of happiness and relief prick at his eyes. He decided Mister P. was the best friend anyone could have. And perhaps Austin was going to turn out to be a best friend too—at least in Joe's new life.

CHAPTER 16

STARTING AND DEPARTING

School had been closed all day on Monday due to the **extreme weather conditions**. So on Tuesday, when everyone was back at their desks, there were many stories to be told—but none as exciting as Austin and Joe's.

Mister P. sat quietly as Austin explained how the bear had helped keep them alive and how they had all been rescued. Joe was proud of Mister P.—really proud—and he told the class about what he had learned on the trip to the lake—about fishing, survival, and friendship.

At the end, Austin grabbed Joe's hand and

Mister P.'s paw and lifted them high in the air. "These guys are legends," he said, and everyone cheered.

Joe knew he was blushing. He gave Austin a friendly punch on the arm. "You're not so bad yourself," he said and drew a small smiley face with his finger.

Mister P. lifted one paw and drew a smiley face with his claw which made everybody laugh.

Later on, when they were all at lunch, Austin told the band about Joe's ukulele playing.

"He's coming along quite well," said Austin, trying to sound serious and keep a straight face. "You can actually recognize the tune he is trying to play!"

"I don't know," said Lettie, her eyes twinkling. "It sounds like he may be a bit too good for us. I mean we don't want to ruin our reputation of being terrible."

"No, no, it's fine," said Joe, also using his most serious voice. "I'll just play really, really badly. I won't let you down, I promise."

"Good, well, that's settled then," said Buzz. "You're definitely in."

Joe took a deep breath. "If you like, you could all come over to my house at the weekend and we could have a practice session—I mean, just so we make sure we can sound as awful as possible."

He waited. He didn't know what he was going to do if they said no.

"Great idea," they all said, and Joe was happy he'd asked and even happier they'd agreed. He reminded himself that this wasn't his band and that he mustn't be bossy like Suzy. He'd go with the flow. He already knew it was going to be fun. He didn't have to stop playing the guitar, but where was the harm in having a bundle of laughs with a bunch of friends?

* * *

Saturday came. Mom fussed around getting food and drinks and tidying the house.

"You don't need to try too hard," said Joe. "I just want it to seem normal. These are my friends, not special guests."

Mom stopped midway through mopping the kitchen floor. She nodded. "Still," she said, "I do need to keep on top of clearing up all that polar bear fur. Talking of which, have you seen Mister P.?"

Joe went through to his room and found Mister P. straightening all his bits and pieces into his suitcase.

"Not you as well," said Joe. "How come everyone is on a straightening mission today?"

Mister P. turned his head, closed the lid of his suitcase and snapped the latches shut, then rubbed his paws together.

"And if you think we're off on another adventure to the lake, think again." Joe smiled. "I'm not going back up there until the summer—in fact, not EVER—unless it's in a helicopter."

Mister P. hung his head and lay down on the floor.

"Cheer up, friend. The others will be here soon."

Mister P. raised his eyes to meet Joe's and then dropped them again. Joe stroked the soft fur on the top of the bear's head and wondered if he was worried about the others coming round. Sometimes it was hard to guess what a polar bear was thinking.

If he was honest, Joe had to admit that he was a little bit nervous about having everyone over.

But he needn't have worried because as soon as they all arrived, the fun started. As for the band sounding terrible—there was no need to worry about that either. They were about the **worst** Joe had ever heard. Which made everything even funnier.

Poor Mister P. sat in the corner with his paws over his ears, and every now and again he held his head as if it really ached. Eventually they took pity on him and Austin handed his ukulele over to Joe.

"We could do with some help," he said quietly. "We would quite like to get a *bit* better."

Joe started with some simple chords and soon the band was sounding more tuneful. Mister P.

started to nod his head and before long they'd almost managed to start playing a recognizable song! Joe gave them all a fist bump.

"Woohoo!" cheered Lettie. "Maybe we're not so bad after all. PO-TEN-TIAL! We could even win!"

Joe loved Lettie's hopeful enthusiasm and was about to suggest a regular practice session when the doorbell rang long and hard.

"Uh-oh," said Joe, "That's probably the neighbors complaining about the noise. Wait here and stay quiet."

Joe could hear the others giggling as he made his way to the front door. Mister P. followed Joe out of the room and, for some reason, he decided to bring his suitcase with him.

"Oh, you think we're off on another adventure, do you? Just because Dad got the truck back this morning doesn't mean we're heading off again. Getting stuck once was enough."

Mister P. looked at him sadly.

As Joe and Mister P. arrived at the front door, Mom was already opening it. Joe didn't recognize the man on the other side or the van parked on the road. He did, however, recognize the bag by the man's side. It was his bag—the one that had gone missing at the airport.

"Delivery for Joe Beechcroft," said the man.

"Wow," said Joe. "I didn't think I was going to see that again."

"Nor me," said Mom. "I'd almost forgotten about it."

"Sign here," said the man, handing Mom a form. "And here please," he said handing her another. Mom signed without really looking. "Is the bear ready?" he asked.

"The *bear*?" said Mom.

The man looked at the form that Mom had just signed.

"It says here, one polar bear for delivery to the port."

"The port?" said Mom. "I'm not sure what you mean."

Joe moved forward and snatched the form from the man's hand. His eyes widened in horror as he read the words.

"Mom," he whispered, "what have you done?"

Mom shook her head, confused.

Joe looked at Mister P. who was sitting quietly, staring sadly at his suitcase.

"That's the one," the man said, pointing at the bear. "I think we might need a cage. Do you have one?"

"Mister P. does *not* need a cage," said Joe. "He lives here with us and he's not going anywhere."

Mister P. picked up his suitcase and handed it to the man. On the suitcase was a large label. The man read it out loud, comparing it to the paperwork.

LIGHTHOUSE
COTTAGES

"NO!" shouted Joe. "No that's wrong. It should say 44 Pinewood Avenue."

"Not according to this," said the man, holding up his clipboard and the suitcase at the same time. "This all matches up perfectly. And signed by Mrs. Beechcroft."

"Well, she can un-sign it."

Dad joined them at the door. "Tell him, Dad," pleaded Joe. "Tell him Mister P. isn't going anywhere. Mom didn't mean to sign."

Dad looked at the form and looked at the label on Mister P.'s case and then looked at Mister P. There was a long silence, then Dad took Joe's hand.

"I think the time has come for Mister P. to move on," he said. "I suppose we knew he wasn't going to stay for ever."

"No we didn't," said Joe, shaking Dad's hand away. "He can't leave. I mean, how are we going to survive without him?"

Mister P. put a paw on Joe's shoulder and

turned his snout towards Joe's bedroom door. Joe could see all his new friends standing in the doorway. He swallowed then leant his forehead against Mister P.'s shoulder, feeling the bear's warm fur against his skin. "You can't go," said Joe. "I won't let you. We all want you to stay. Not just me." The bear rested his chin on top of Joe's head and neither of them moved.

"Come along now," said the delivery man, not unkindly. "This bear has got a boat to catch."

Mister P. gave a big sigh, stood up, and walked slowly out of the door. He stopped at the top of the ramp, turned, and gave Joe a small nod. Then he walked down the ramp after the delivery man and climbed into the back of his van.

Joe's throat tightened as he watched the van pull away, and his eyes burned as he tried to hold back the tears. Austin, Lettie, Conrad, and Buzz gathered round him.

"We can't let him leave alone," said Austin. "We should go to the port and give him a proper send-off. You've got your truck back haven't you?"

"It'll be a squish," said Dad.

There was no time to argue. Everyone jumped into the truck, some in the front and some in the back. Joe strapped himself in and Dad drove to the port as fast as he could.

There was a ship waiting at the dockside, loaded up with huge containers of every color. As they ran towards the pier, they could see Mister P. making his way up the gangplank and onto the deck.

The gangplank lifted behind him and the ship gave one long blast of its horn.

Peeeeeep!

Slowly, slowly, the ship edged away from the dock. Mister P. stood at the rail, his paw raised high in the air.

"Goodbye, Mister P. Goodbye!" everyone shouted. Everyone except Joe. Joe couldn't speak. He didn't take his eyes off the huge bear who was gradually shrinking as the ship made its way out towards the ocean. Joe watched until Mister P. was a tiny pinprick in the distance.

The others turned to go back to the car, but Joe couldn't bring himself to move. A cold wind blew down from the mountains. Joe opened his hands, caught the breeze and closed them again.

"Goodbye, Mister P.," he whispered into his cupped hands. "Thank you." Then he opened his hands once more and let the words blow away across the waves towards the ship. He knew his message would get to the bear. He just knew it. A few random snowflakes fell from the gray sky and Joe wiped them from his cheeks. He would never forget Mister P.

Joe headed back to join the others in the warmth of the truck. He was so numb with sadness that he hadn't even noticed his goosebumps or how violently he was shivering.

He took one last look over his shoulder. He knew he had to let Mister P. go. And his new friends were waiting for him. And he would be all right.

CHAPTER 17
ENDS AND FRIENDS

The journey home was quiet. The truck felt strange without Mister P. and the house felt strange without Mister P. Everywhere Joe looked there seemed to be a large, Mister-P-sized hole. He was glad the others were with him. It helped to fill the space and cheer him up.

Dad came in waving his phone. "You're not going to believe this," he said, "but our container of stuff from home arrived on Mister P.'s ship. You'll soon have *all* your things back again."

"Do you think Mister P. will ever come back?" asked Austin.

"No," said Joe, very seriously. "I think it was too cold for him here. He's probably gone off for a vacation on the beach or something. I expect he's lying around on a sun bed drinking cocktails."

The others looked thoughtful. Then Austin's face cracked into a smile and they all burst into fits of laughter.

* * *

The band competition was almost a triumph. **The Blizzards** decided to go all out to win and made a cool set with paintings of snowdrifts and pine trees and a large polar bear. They'd practiced until their fingers nearly dropped off. They dressed in their onesie snowsuits and woolly hats and nearly baked. Okay, if Joe was honest, they weren't exactly perfect (him included) but they were happy and that seemed to make everyone else happy. The audience definitely liked them the best—they were all on their feet, clapping and cheering.

The judges said it was a HARD decision (judges always say that) and then awarded the prize to Mitchell's band and put **The Blizzards** in second place.

Joe went over to Mitchell and shook his hand. "Congratulations," he said. "That was really good."

"Thanks," said Mitchell. "I think you got the audience vote and that's the one that really counts."

Mitchell moved to one side and beckoned Joe to follow him. "Someone told me you play guitar very well," he said. "I just wondered if you'd like to hang out sometime."

"Yeah," said Joe. "Why not? In fact, we're heading back to my place now for a coming-second celebration. You could all join us if you wanted."

"And hang out with a bunch of ukulele players?" said Mitchell, raising an eyebrow.

Joe raised an eyebrow back. "A bunch of BAD ukulele players," he corrected him and laughed.

"Sounds like a good plan," said Mitchell. "Sure. That'd be cool."

* * *

This was Joe's new world. Except suddenly it didn't seem so new any more. He missed his old home but he liked his new one too. He'd never forget Mister P. and he'd never forget his old friends. And when the time came for him to leave, he'd never forget his new friends either.

MISTER P.'S SNOW STORM SURVIVAL GUIDE

Remember!
YOU ARE NOT A POLAR BEAR.
It's difficult to survive outdoors during a snowstorm, so stay with your car for shelter and protection.

It's important to unclog snow from a vehicle's exhaust pipe regularly. Most polar bears can help with this, but if there are none around, you will have to do it yourself.

Remove ice and snow from around your vehicle. If you don't have big polar bear paws, you can use a shovel.

🐾 Polar bears have two layers of fur to keep them cozy in the cold, but humans need to layer up in warm clothing.

🐾 Polar bears don't need to drink much water, but humans do—always make sure you have some with you in the car in case you get stranded.

🐾 If you don't have a Mister P. to cuddle up with, make sure you pack a warm blanket.

🐾 A polar bear has huge feet so that they can they can easily walk on snow and ice, but make sure you have a pair of boots with good grip!

Mister P. attracts lots of attention, but if you're missing a polar bear, try creating an SOS sign in the snow.

Mister P. may be able to bring you some raw fish, but would you really want to eat it? Better to pack some tasty snacks instead!

Remember, you shouldn't really leave the house if there's a bad storm coming. Stay inside with your polar bear best friend instead.

ABOUT THE AUTHOR

Maria Farrer lives in a small village in the Yorkshire Dales, England, with her husband and her very spoiled dog. She used to live on a small farm in New Zealand with a flock of sheep, a herd of cows, two badly behaved pigs, and a budgie that sat on her head while she wrote. She trained as a speech therapist and teacher and later she completed an MA in Writing for Young People. She loves language and enjoys reading and writing books for children of all ages. She likes to ride her bike to the top of steep hills so she can hurtle back down again as fast as possible. She also loves mountains, snow, and adventure and one day she dreams of going to the Arctic to see polar bears in the wild.

ABOUT THE ILLUSTRATOR

Daniel Rieley is a British freelance illustrator based in Lisbon. After studying at The Arts Institute, Bournemouth, undertaking an epic backpacking adventure in Australia, and working for three years in London, he decided to take off to sunny Portugal. For the past few years, Daniel has been working on several illustration projects from advertising, print, and card design to children's books.

When Daniel is not drawing, you can probably find him trying to catch waves, taking photos with old cameras, or playing his newly discovered sport, Padel.